Unveiled Love

A Benton Center Romance

David Allen Edmonds

Copyright 2024 by David Allen Edmonds

Published by Snowbelt Publishing Ltd.

ISBN -13: 978-0-9985466-5-0 (paperback)
ISBN -13: 978-0-9985466-4-3 (e-book)

Editing: Dr. Stacey Gnall
Cover: Rachel Fox www.rachfoxdesign.com
Layout and formatting: Inkling Creative Strategies
www.inklingcreative.work
Readers: Barbara Kauffman, Paula Lynn, Connie Ray-
buck, Paul Kubis

Dedication

To the librarians and booksellers of
America, and to those who value democracy
enough to work for it.

Chapter 1

The farther Kennedy Philips jogged away from the Square and down the slope to the river, the better she felt. Each stride on the crunchy stone path invigorated the long muscles of her legs, and each breath she drew rejuvenated her. She was confident when she ran, her mind and body in synch, her doubts pushed aside. This time her plan would work.

The path wound around leafing maples and oaks, through bushes budding tentatively in the faint April sun. It was cool, but she was comfortable running, and safer the farther she got from the town above and behind her. Her shoes crunched on the gravel as the path opened to reveal the stone bridge arching over the river.

At the low point of the trail, she thought to stop again on the bridge, but kept her pace steady. She would admire the gurgling water later, after she weathered the criticism. Maybe drop a twig or a leaf into the stream and watch it work its way through the boulders and rocks. Her reward after working through the next couple of hours. A private reward as she had no one to share it with. She took a deep breath at the far side of the bridge and measured it out.

It was dark along the river, the foliage dense even in the early spring. A pair of women coming toward her continued talking and didn't return her wave. She passed another jogger going her way, but as the slope began climbing up toward Benton Center, she was alone.

The incline steepened the closer she got to town; she shortened her stride and pounded her feet into the path. She breathed harder but continued her steady pace. Alone in Benton Center, she knew the feeling. Always the outsider. The odd one, the one that didn't fit. She'd tried, really tried to make the town like her, even to just accept her. To see her for who she really was. But they had seen only what they wanted to see, and she had left the small town, the gossipers, the strivers, and the cliques. They had never given her a chance. That was six months ago and now she was back.

The path crested and revealed the Benton Center Town Square. The Gazebo as its hub, and the eight white walkways its spokes. The benches in the grass, the shops lining the four sides. The Town Hall, the church, the courthouse. It was beautiful and charming, but for her, beautiful, charming, and painful. She stopped and lifted her foot onto a park bench.

She re-tied the safety yellow lace in her Asics Magic Speed running shoe. The silly color didn't quite match her City Grit Green Lululemon tights, or her fluorescent headband, and she didn't care. Her days of trying to appease them by being Barbie perfect were behind her. She swallowed her fears with another cleansing breath and willed herself to walk calmly through the Square to the Pot & Flagon beyond. She was absolutely sure they were watching her from the bay window.

Chapter 2

Chris Lennox maneuvered another pile of debris onto the dustpan and into the black plastic bag. There has to be a joke about this, he thought as he twisted the tie, but couldn't quite find it. Something about ten pounds of trash in a five-pound bag. He propped the broom on the partition wall and stretched the kink out of his back.

He was nearing the end of several stressful weeks and still telling himself he had made the right decision. The good way of thinking about it was downsizing, making his business leaner, nimbler, and more able to pivot in today's challenging small business economy. The bad way, and the way most of the ladies in the Pot & Flagon kept reminding him, was that he was giving up on the family business. No, he'd told them, I'm dodging a bullet. I'm keeping the store open and receiving a healthy amount of rent. Some of them actually agreed.

What that came down to was stuffing the Lennox Family Bookshop into a space half the size and renting the space to the Rassmussen For Senate campaign. That's it, he thought as the joke occurred to him; ten pounds of books into a five-pound bag. Not even remotely funny.

He picked up the trash bag and the broom and took a last look at the nearly empty store front. Folding tables leaned against the far wall next to a stack of metal chairs. He'd left the cork boards hanging on the bare brick walls, thinking they could be used by his tenants. Rectangles of darker color marked the cork where he'd removed the layers of flyers and postings. Those and the school kids' artworks were balled up in one of the many black bags the one in his hand was waiting to join. His eyes once again tracked the lines of the heavy crown molding and the picture rail until they stopped abruptly at the newly constructed partition wall bisecting the space. Hopefully this was a temporary fix, and he could reconnect the decorative wood by the end of the year.

His grandfather, the first Christopher Lennox in Benton Center, was an avid reader and sold books and stationery in his general store. He was so successful the bookstore soon replaced the groceries, hardware and dry goods. The third Christopher Lennox exited the empty side, locked the door, and entered the now crowded bookstore. In the last several years his book sales had fallen off, and he might have to consider an offer from a chain store to buy him out. The money from the lease was enough to postpone that painful decision for the moment.

Every inch of space was taken up with bookshelves: massive, dark stained wooden pieces of furniture, overstuffed with books. The aisles between them were wide enough for one person to pass, barely. As he struggled with the trash bag and broom, he couldn't help but think how comfortable the old space had been. As it was now, he hadn't even been able to fit in all the shelves; several of the massive units stood empty in the back room. He managed to save one chair and floor lamp, now sitting alone at the edge of the front window. The other chairs, the sofas and the game tables were stacked in the back, the ones that didn't take the ride to the dump.

Chris had hired movers and begged friends to move the books and the shelves from one side to the other over the last several weekends. He'd left the cleanup for himself. It was easy enough, and he had tired of their endless suggestions to improve his business. He tossed the trash bag onto the loading dock in the back with the others.

The book business was bad in small towns nationally, everyone losing market share to the big boys and the internet. Learning from COVID, he'd kept the store open as much as he could during the move, fearing the worst if he closed even for a day. It had helped, but his sales hadn't returned to their pre-COVID numbers.

He slumped into the office chair. His grandfather's, then his father's, now his. He loved the ancient green leather; it was like sitting in a giant first baseman's mitt. He closed the computer and picked up the two envelopes. One was from BazillionBooks, the other from the Scott Rasmussen campaign. The former a sellout, the latter a lifeline.

Maybe he had that reversed. He didn't know, but at least he had solved the problem for now. The store was still open, his name was still above the door, and he'd absorbed the loss of his only fulltime employee. He and his third cousin Chloe could manage the smaller space. Would have to.

He sighed and checked the time on the huge Regulator wall clock. Someone from the campaign was supposed to be here by now. It would be just his luck they were going to cancel, and he'd downsized for nothing but the small down payment. He hoped not.

Chapter 3

As the seat of Conway County, Benton Center, Ohio, holds significant political power. As the center of the town, the Square holds some power as well. The courts and the commissioners' offices are directly on the square, as are two major banks, and the farmers exchange is just down the street. But if you were to ask a pair of residents where the real power lay, she would point to the coffee shop and tell you about the Gossip Club, and he would merely know where to get a good cup of coffee and a sticky bun.

Kennedy pushed the button and the crossing lights flashed excitedly. The bay window of the Pot & Flagon seemed to reach out to her through the traffic like a big-eyed bug. She forced out a breath and strode quickly into the crosswalk. She would not let the Benton Center Gossip Club get to her again.

Teddi Burns was filling the display case with bear claws and didn't look up as the bell over the door tinkled. The owner of the coffee shop looked as she always did, busy, with a brightly colored turban on her head that nearly matched the variegated apron stretched around her ample waist. The tables in the front portion of the room were more than half filled. The music room/wine bar through the arch in back was dark.

As Teddi pulled out the now empty tray and straightened up, she said "Now look what the cat dragged in."

Kennedy grinned. "Good to see you again, Ms. Burns." She thought to give the older woman a hug but was on the wrong side of the counter and the woman's hands were full. Maybe later.

Teddi set down the tray and wiped her hands on a towel. "What brings you back to town? Thought you were some big muckety-muck in Columbus."

Kennedy couldn't tell if the lines around the Black woman's mouth were forming a smile, or she was being mocked. "No, not me," she replied brightly. "But Senator Rasmussen is kind of a big deal. The Party thinks highly of him."

Teddi smiled a little. "Is he now?"

Kennedy leaned forward as if conspiring. "He thinks he is."

Teddi laughed as she came around the counter and enveloped Kennedy in a hug. "Good to see you back where you belong."

"Me too." The younger woman felt as if she'd passed an algebra test. She took a step back and nodded her head at the tableful of women in the bay window. "Is that what they think?"

"Probably not, but you'll set them straight, I bet." Teddi bustled back to her post. "Your usual?"

"You remembered?" Kennedy heard the high pitch of her voice and reminded herself to tone it down. It's another thing the Ladies would find childish, or worse, fake.

"Honey, no one around here orders a latte with as many directions as you." She began writing on the side of a paper cup. "Let's see, decaf, no sugar, oat milk, shot of?"

"Pumpkin Spice?" Kennedy arched her eyebrows hopefully.

"It's April, young lady. You know you gotta wait." The barista whooshed steam into the mug and set it next to an enormous cinnamon muffin on the counter. "Vanilla."

"Thank you." Kennedy gestured again at the Gossip Club. "Pretty quiet today."

"Got a serious issue to discuss," Teddi said and pointed to an open place at the table. The ladies sat in large wooden chairs; the backless stool was for witnesses or defendants.

Kennedy reminded herself she had nothing to feel guilty for, then questioned a look at Teddi. "Serious issue," the barista said. "You shouldn't just jump on in. Got to do with the schools."

"Don't they need your advice?"

"Don't you worry about that, honey, I let my feelings be known." She punched an order into the computer with one hand and waved the other at a customer. "Thanks for coming in, Clarissa. See you again tomorrow."

KK took a bite of the muffin and snuck a glance at the table in the front window. A slim, dark-haired woman was standing up and nodding at the group of faces. She guessed the woman was saying goodbye.

Teddi returned. "Looks like they're ready for you, Kennedy. Good luck."

Kennedy picked up her plate and latte. She wasn't going to the dentist or being called to the principal's office, but it felt like it. I'm a grown woman, she told herself, it's just that they are so judgmental. They never liked me; they never gave me a chance. I have to show them who I really am.

Seven women sat at the oval wooden table in the window. One chair was free, and she headed for it. She recognized most of them; the younger ones, Maggie Wellover and Sammi Yoder, had been classmates. Another, Gena Cobb, was Mayor Grieselhuber's secretary. Mary Jane's daughter was a friend of Teddi's nephew. How did she remember that? The other faces were familiar, but she couldn't remember their names.

All seven faces were turned to her. Kennedy put on a brave smile and sat down. "Ladies, it's great to see you all again."

"Are you moving back?"

"Did the senator fire you?"

"Why are you dressed like that?"

"Yeah, where are your heels?"

"Nothing's pink."

The questions themselves didn't bother Kennedy, she'd expected them, but they revealed the attitude that she'd expected as well. The Ladies didn't see themselves as anything other than good citizens. Not busybodies or blabbermouths, gaining and sharing tidbits was crucial to making informed decisions. They considered themselves essential to the democratic process.

Kennedy finished chewing. She dabbed her mouth with a napkin and fixed her smile. *Nothing has changed, not one damn thing. To them I'm still Airhead Barbie.* She took a cleansing breath and made sure to look each woman at the table in the eye. "I bring you an invitation."

"I bet I know what it is," Sammi said. Her bright eyes sparkled, and she clasped her hands together. Unlike the others, the owner of the Dress Shop had neither a plate full of muffin remnants in front of her nor a negative attitude. She poked through her purse and held up a set of keys.

Kennedy nodded. "You're right. I bet those are the keys for the empty store front?"

Gena directed her stare at Kennedy. "The bookstore, you mean. You're the one who's running the Lennox family out of business."

"It's my understanding that the bookstore is still open, still in business. He's downsizing." Kennedy looked at Sammi, who nodded, but didn't speak. "I'm, we're, renting the space. For the campaign, Senator Rasmussen's campaign."

"Does the family want to downsize?" Gena continued staring.

Kennedy clasped her hands together in her lap. "I don't know, Ms. Cobb. The senator wants a presence in Conway County, so I contacted the Chamber of Commerce. I knew a place on the Square would be best, and they said it was available."

Sammi jingled the keys. "Come on, KK, we can take a look." She started to rise, but Kennedy laid a hand on her forearm. Sammi noticed the polish on KK's thumb was scratched off.

"No, let's get this straight." Kennedy returned Gena's stare and said as calmly as she could, "I work for the Rasmussen campaign for the US Senate. I'm on Scott's staff as well."

"He's a Senator now you said." This from a pinch-faced, pasty looking woman.

"Scott is a member of the Ohio Senate now. He's running for the US Senate in Washington." Kennedy fought the urge to scream at her ignorance and managed to keep her pitch low and her smile steady.

"That's confusing," the woman muttered.

Mary Jane whispered to Gena, "She called him Scott."

Kennedy ignored them. "So, yeah, it's temporary, six months max, then the bookstore can have the space back."

Maggie shot Gena and Mary Jane a look and cleared her voice. "I didn't expect to see you again so soon, KK."

"I didn't expect it either." Kennedy looked at her former rival's wavy auburn hair with envy. "But the campaign decided it's a good move, so here I am."

"This is about your father isn't it." Gena's stare now lost any semblance of warmth. "About BiggInsCo's money and political clout."

"Well, Daddy's a Republican, and he usually donates, so——"

"——so Rasmussen picked you to reach into Daddy's wallet. How convenient." Gena smirked and looked around the group for agreement. Several heads bobbed. Mary Jane shook her head but didn't speak.

"That's rude, Ms. Cobb," Sammi squeaked. Teddi stood silently behind her.

Kennedy laughed. "Well, that's the answer to the first question I came in here with. No, you bunch haven't changed." Now Sammi laid her hand on KK's arm.

Kennedy pulled her hand away and waved it like Queen Elizabeth. "You all still think I'm just Daddy's little girl. I get it, it's a role I have played." She turned to Sammi and Teddi. "That's why I came in here today, and that's why I'll come back. I don't need your permission, Ms. Cobb. I want to show you that I am capable of doing things on my own.

"In that regard——" She warmed her gaze and looked at each in turn. "I am inviting all of you to the opening of the Rasmussen for Senate campaign headquarters." Before she could stop herself, she added, "You know where it is, right down the block."

"All the books are gone, and the kids' artwork," the pinch-faced woman hissed. "There's nothing in there but dust."

"My team and I will have that taken care of, Ma'am." She showed them an even larger smile. "Light hors d'oeuvres and wine, also." She paused and decided to take a small shot. "For the adults, of course."

No comments this time. Kennedy rose and Sammi followed. "Hope to see you ladies there. You know, you are very influential in BenCen, and it would be great for our campaign if you'd attend."

As they left the Pot & Flagon, Sammi grinned. "That went well, don't you think? You even complimented them."

Kennedy shook her head and scraped furiously at her thumb.

Chapter 4

Kennedy shortened her stride so the petite Sammi Yoder could keep up. "How's the business going?" She gestured toward the purple-ish Victorian building on the far side of the Square. "I really like those colors."

Sammi looked up from her purse with another set of keys in her hand. "Really well. Thanks for asking."

"And Arjun and Riya? Are they doing OK?"

"My parents?" Sammi beamed. "It's good that I'm at the store full time. They're getting so they can't work a whole day anymore."

"But they can't step away, can they." Kennedy grinned. "It's a family trait."

"Workaholics. You know us well." Sammi smiled at the taller woman before turning and jiggling the key into the lock on the bookstore door.

The door protested but grudgingly opened to reveal the future Rasmussen For Senate campaign headquarters. Kennedy followed her guide inside. "Pretty good size."

"It seemed so much smaller with all the books. Much larger than I thought" Sammi's brow furrowed. "Not quite clean yet."

"Picture rail, some tables and chairs, corkboards." Kennedy looked at Sammi. "Suppose we can use them?"

"That's why Chris left them, sure. You remember him, right?"

"Look at the ceiling!" Kennedy pirouetted and pointed her hand up. "That's tin, right, pressed tin? Must be 150 years old. Ooh, maybe it's copper. It's kinda that color."

"I think so, it's beautiful."

Kennedy stopped spinning to see Sammi at the door, the other set of keys in her hand. "These are for the BNB. The address is on the tab, it's across from the hardware store."

"Aren't you going to stay and help move the furniture?" Kennedy held her hand out for the keys and grinned.

"Nope, I'm your Chamber of Commerson person and friendly guide, but I don't do the heavy lifting." Sammi returned the smile and her brown eyes sparkled.

Despite the way she was treated for marrying Irv Yoder, she is the friendliest, most positive person in the whole town, Kennedy thought. If she could survive the Gossip Club, I can too. She grinned. "You got people to do that for you, right?"

A blush darkened Sammi's light brown skin and framed her wide smile. "And a nervous doctor." She framed her hands around her abdomen.

"I'm so happy for you!" Kennedy held open her arms.

"Five months tomorrow!" Sammi's voice was muffled by the hug. Kennedy rocked her for a moment, then extended her arms. "Now get out of here and get off your feet, Momma."

"I will, I will." Sammi turned at the door. "You sound like my mother."

Chris Lennox used his butt to hold open the door to his side of the building and maneuvered the sandwich board through the narrow gap. Sammi brushed past him as she raced out the other door. The door that used to be part of his bookstore. Harsh laughter, more like the cackling of a witch, chased her out onto the sidewalk and down the street.

He was due to meet the contact person from Rassmussen's campaign, and the nicest person in town is running away? Chris set the triangular message board in place, more in front of his side than where he used to set it. He peered into the vacant side as more laughing billowed out the open door. He hesitated, then stepped inside. "Everything OK in here?"

Kennedy was slowly rotating, laughing to herself while looking up. "I love this ceiling. Is it tin or copper?"

"I heard cackling or shrieking, I thought someone was in distress." Chris shook his head at the sight of the empty room.

"What? Oh, you must be my landlord." Kennedy dropped her arms and appeared to awaken. "You must think I'm crazy."

Chris found himself in Rick's Bar in *Casablanca*. Kennedy Phillips. Anyone but her.

The brows above his hazel eyes grew into a knot. "What did you say to poor Samantha? She ran out of here as if escaping with her life."

"No worries. That girl is full of life." Kennedy strode to him, extending her hand. "Kennedy Phillips. My secretary spoke to you on the phone."

He shook her hand then dropped it. "I know who you are."

"Your tenant. And I just love this space."

She hasn't changed a bit. Still has no idea who I am. "Good. I do too."

She pulled her eyes from his and spoke to the ceiling. "It's gorgeous, and large, it's a, well, spacious space."

Chris saw only the truncated molding and temporary partition. Of all the gin joints in all the world, it had to be Kennedy Phillips. "Well said."

"You must think I'm a loon." Kennedy arranged her clothes and her expression.

No, stuck up, opinionated and self-centered. "I'm just here to see if you need anything. And to find out what made Sammi go running out of here."

"Wait, you think I chased her away?" Kennedy laughed. "No, I just congratulated her on being pregnant."

"She's pregnant?" Chris shook his head. He never noticed that kind of thing.

"Probably due around the election. Yeah, so I was laughing about her giving birth to a human being, and the voters giving birth to a new Senator and this space being—"

"—spacious?"

Her eyes widened. "That's it, exactly."

"As you said before."

"I did?"

He managed to not say something regrettable. Something exactly right, but regrettable. He needed the rent money. "If you, uh, need anything, I'm right on the other side of the partition."

"The great Wall of Benton Center?"

"Not even close." He held up a key. "Here's two more keys, an extra front, and one for the back."

She approached and held out her hand. "Berlin Wall?"

What was the matter with this woman? "Nope." He dropped the keys into her hand. "You don't remember me, do you? Chris Lennox?"

Dimpled chin, curly brown hair, hazel eyes. She had no idea. Her face flushed. "Sure. Sure I do."

"No, you don't."

"No, I do, we, were, high school."

"Good guess but that's all it is. I wasn't cool enough for you to know."

Kennedy's mind raced. She knew everybody, but. Her face brightened. "Lab partners. Biology lab, sophomore year."

Chris shook his head. "Nice try, homecoming queen." He spun away. At the door he muttered, "And Pumpkin Queen."

The door banged shut. Darn it, she thought, I manage to get through the coffee shop interrogation, and some nerd shows up who thinks he knows me. No one around here knows me. She snorted a sharp breath, inhaled slowly, then took in her surroundings. But I got things going, and I'm not going to let anyone stop me. I'm not.

Next door Chris flopped into the one remaining easy chair. The Rich and Famous. I can't rub two nickels together and she can just flounce in here and take half of my bookstore. My family's bookstore.

He let his eyes wander across the Square in front of him. And I can't say anything. I need her and the campaign money. He looked up as the door opened and a woman took a tentative step inside.

"Are you still in business?"

"That I am, Mrs. Finch." My first customer of the day, he thought. "A little cramped, but still in business."

She hesitated and pointed to her left. "But the other side?"

"Temporary situation." He led her into the narrow stacks. "The Romance books are down this aisle. I got the new Colleen Hoover for you." Hopefully not my only customer.

Chapter 5

Her cell chirped, and Kennedy checked it. The communications truck with the computers and phones was circling the Square trying to find her location. She clicked off and hurried out onto the sidewalk where Chris was talking with an older woman. Kennedy shook her head and wondered why she'd pretended to remember him from high school. What was the point? She spotted the panel truck with the Rasmussen for Senate signage and waved them down.

"You're right on time, Alvin," she called as the driver lowered the passenger-side window.

"Can I park here?"

"I checked with the city. As long as we're loading or unloading, we have forty minutes."

"On the ball as usual, Boss." Alvin opened the rear doors and pulled out a hand truck. "We all set inside?"

"Wait till you see the space." She held open the door as the young Black man wheeled several boxes into the store front. "It's huge," he said.

Kennedy helped the team set up the folding tables and bring in the remaining equipment. They would set up the phone bank along the brick wall where they could use the corkboards. Workstations for the volunteers would be grouped in the center. Her desk and pseudo-office were in the rear.

Alvin crawled out from under one of the tables and said, "I got it from here, Ms. Phillips." Kennedy laughed. "I am at the end of my expertise. Be sure to lock up when you're done."

"Will do. See you tomorrow with the rest of the stuff." He disappeared under the table. The volunteers and the rest of her staff would arrive then, too. Kennedy nodded. Her plans were unfolding according to schedule.

The BNB Sammi had arranged for her was indeed across the street from the hardware store. A narrow, three-story brick building, four if you counted the apartment a half flight below street level. She climbed the half flight up and unlocked the front door.

Her rooms were up a skinny staircase, one in the front, the other down the hall. She chose the street side room and hefted her suitcase onto the brass bed. It bounced happily and she grinned at the thought of falling asleep in the feathery softness. She pulled back the curtains on the tall, narrow window and peered through the wavy glass onto the street below. Next to the hardware store was the new Mexican restaurant. She thought Scott would like it.

She took the keyring from the small table by the door and walked down the hall to the rear-facing room. It was similar to hers, a bit smaller, and the view of the library and old elementary school was charming. Not that Scott would notice it. She'd taken Sammi's advice and taken two rooms instead of one; she didn't need to give them anything more to talk about.

She plopped onto the bed in her room and called him on her cell. It beeped, but he didn't answer. Busy, she thought, and pulled off her running clothes. She didn't understand why the gossip ladies had so much power in Benton Center, but she had stood her ground. Meeting Lennox on the other hand had been a disaster. Why had she pretended to know him? She let out her frustration with a long sigh. She would settle her nerves tomorrow with a run. For now, she'd shower and change before meeting her father at the club. A fresh coat of nail polish would help too.

As the President and CEO of BiggInsCo, Grantham Phillips of course had his own parking space, a primo spot close to the front entrance with his name engraved on a small, tasteful sign. But the main building was several blocks from the Golf Club, so Kennedy pulled up the gently curved drive and availed herself of the valet service. She had parked her car in the nearby lot once before, and the embarrassment for her father had been unbearable.

She checked herself in the rearview as the valet opened her door. She had his tip ready and clicked across the wide walkway and up the steps. She thanked the young man holding the shiny green door. "Right this way, Ms. Kennedy, your father is waiting."

"His usual table, Juan?"

The maître d' lowered his voice. "His only table."

They wound their way through the partially filled dining room, candles flickering on white linen tablecloths, flatware sparkling on dark green napkins. In a private alcove in the back corner, Grantham stood up and extended his hand. "Daughter."

"Father." She pecked his cheek and they both sat down. He spread the enormous napkin across his lap. Grantham

Phillips was a ruddy faced, white-haired gentleman, at ease both in corporate boardrooms and lavish locker rooms, comfortable gloating with peers about his vast fortune, or playing the common man and keeping it out of sight. He smiled at his only child. "Very nice to see you, Kennedy, very nice."

She squeezed his hand. "Me, too."

Juan re-appeared with the leather-bound menus. Grantham laid them aside. "I'll have the sirloin. The usual way."

"Yessir, Mr. Phillips."

"And my daughter will have the shrimp stir-fry."

Kennedy wanted to be furious. She was a grown woman and could order for herself, but darn, that's exactly what she wanted to have. "I will," she said. "And a glass of Riesling, please."

Juan bowed and retreated. She shook her head. "How do you always know?"

"I'm your father."

She couldn't suppress her grin. "At least you didn't use your Darth Vader voice."

"Luuuke," he began, then snorted.

They both laughed at their favorite joke. He sipped his scotch, and said, "So how is life in Columbus, the political hub of the Western World."

"Hopefully we'll find out how life is in DC."

He raised his eyebrows. "It's going that well?"

"It's always about the primary in Ohio, and we're polling well. You never know, but signs are good." She gave his hand another quick squeeze. "And thank you for your help."

He nodded. "Are you using McKenzie? He's top-notch."

"I took your advice. Best pollster I ever worked with.

Scott loves him."

Grantham swallowed some scotch. "If the numbers are what he wants to hear, he'd love a chimpanzee. Any politician would."

To Kennedy's ear, it sounded like "politician" was a dread disease. "Scott's not like that, Daddy."

"They're all like that, daughter."

She settled her hands in her lap, carefully keeping the marred thumbs out of sight. "Wait until you meet him. You two should sit down and have a talk. Or the three of us. We can go to the Flagon after the opening."

Juan and a younger man appeared and set the dishes on the table. When they left, Grantham said, "Maybe. We'll see."

That was as good as I'll get, Kennedy thought. She speared a shrimp and a legume and popped them in her mouth. "In any event, we can all meet at the donor event."

The CEO hesitated, then smiled. "The three of us. That will be nice."

Kennedy reached for her wine. "Speaking of which, is there anything I need to do about the venue?"

"I got it covered. Juan and the boys have it all under control."

"I don't need to—"

"—do anything. Like I said." He set down his knife and looked at her.

"I know, I know, you're my dad and—"

"—I'll do what I said I would."

He was right, she knew that, but at the same time, she didn't want to need his help. She was grateful to him, and the campaign certainly was, but she wanted to make her own decisions. She smiled. "Thank you."

"You're welcome." He wiped his mouth and smiled. "It's so nice being able to see you, have dinner, you know like normal folks."

Being careful to keep her voice low and slow, she said, "Daddy, our family is many things, but normal folks is not one of them." She might have overstepped, but he returned her smile.

"I'm not, but it would be great to have you, and dare I say a pack of little ones, around here on a regular basis."

"No, you may not say that, Daddy." She aimed her fork at him. "But it would be nice, I agree."

"I know a guy who could get you a job——"

It was her turn to interrupt. "We've talked about this before." She accented her words by jabbing the fork. "I want to do things on my own."

He grinned. "Within limits."

"Absolutely. Just like you taught me."

He grinned. "Just as I taught you."

"Oh, Daddy."

Chapter 6

Kennedy stabbed off the alarm on her cell and took one last stretch. The fluffy brass bed had been as comfortable as it looked, and she didn't want to leave it. But her set-up team would be arriving in an hour or so, and more importantly, the campaign HQ was her baby and she wanted to be sure the rollout went smoothly.

Scott hadn't called her back, but maybe he sent a text. She rolled to the edge of the bed and checked. "Sorry, babe, way busy. Get some sleep, I'll see you at the ribbon cutting." And a couple of pink hearts. Not much, but at least he'd thought of her. She sighed, then dressed and bounded down the steps and into the street.

Benton Center was cool this morning, but the air fresh and the sky clear, and she had enjoyed her run. As she cooled down, she noticed the big flowerpots in the Square were still unplanted. Northeast Ohio was known for its late April frosts. As she paused beneath the Pot & Flagon sign, she giggled to herself that it would probably be a little frosty inside as well.

Before she could open the coffee shop door, Sammi appeared at her side. "You sure you want to go in there? They were really rude yesterday."

Kennedy gave her a quick hug. "I have to. They think they can push me around, but they can't."

Sammi looked her up and down. "But that's the third outfit you've worn in the last twelve hours. You're just giving them ammunition."

"What? These are workout clothes and work clothes. We're setting up the HQ today." Her face clouded in thought. "OK, running clothes yesterday, nothing pink, but . . . wait, they saw me at dinner last night with my father?"

"The walls have eyes, and so does the Gossip Club." Sammi led her through the tinkly door and into the P&F. Moments later, cinnamon buns and lattes in hand, they found chairs at the big table in the bay window.

The Gossip Club barely acknowledged their arrival. The half dozen pairs of eyes were focused on the dark-haired woman Kennedy had seen leaving yesterday. She was speaking in a nervous whisper, and they had to concentrate to hear.

"—they're making it so hard to teach. I feel like someone's always looking over my shoulder."

"That would be hard, I suppose." Mary Jane furrowed her unibrow.

"But you're a public employee." Gena cocked her head to the side. "You have to expect that, don't you? I know I do."

The woman slung a large bag over her shoulder and picked up her purse. "Maybe so, but I can't teach with someone spying on me, keeping track of every word I say." She stood up. "Sandy, the other second grade teacher, thinks they're listening to her over the loudspeaker. Trying to catch her. Trying to catch both of us." She backed her chair away from the table.

Teddi stood up next to her. "Just do your best, dear." She took her by the arm and led her to the door.

Kennedy questioned a look at Sammi.

"Joanie Kimble, elementary school teacher," Gena responded before Sammi could. "Seems to be having an issue with the chain of authority."

Teddi spoke before sitting back down. "That's not fair. The issue is affecting her students and the way she teaches."

Several heads bobbed in agreement. "They're mostly picture books. There's a million out there, just use different books," the pinch-faced lady said. "That's what I'd do."

Gena agreed. "After all, it's only second grade, right."

Kennedy realized the women were talking about book banning. The Senator had a sheaf of papers dealing with the subject, but as yet hadn't taken a position.

"Only second grade?" Connie Richardson opened her palms as she spoke as if offering her opinion to the table. "That's when they learn to read." Kennedy remembered her as the Latin teacher.

"Meredith learned to read at home, when she was five," Mary Jane stated.

"I don't see what all the fuss is about." The pinch-faced woman set her mug down hard on the table.

"They're taking books out of the classroom," Sammi said. "The curriculum has already been approved here locally, and by the State Board of Ed."

"Well, Mrs. Yoder, I for one am truly bored of education. B-o-r-e-d." Gena got the laugh she craved and nodded around the table. "As for you, Ms. Phillips, what does our State Senator have to say about this issue?"

Kennedy carefully laid the cinnamon bun on the

plate. "He's researching the situation, Ms. Cobb. Doing his due diligence."

"Can't make up his mind, can he." Gena smirked broadly.

"Doesn't want to shoot his mouth off without knowing the facts." Kennedy wanted to add, "Like you do around here," but managed to keep that to herself.

Mary Jane and the pinch-faced woman giggled, and Teddi smiled. Gena saw their reactions and focused on Kennedy's outfit. "Slumming today, are we?"

"Working today at the HQ." Kennedy pushed back from the table. "Left my pink corvette in Columbus."

"I thought the Queen had people to do her work. Minions."

Kennedy didn't want to be goaded, but stood up and said, "A good leader is not afraid to get her hands dirty."

Sammi clapped her hands. "Yes. You go, girl!"

As the door tinkled behind the waving yellow ponytail, Gena said, "Am I missing something? Does that seem to be our Kennedy?"

Chris sensed the presence of someone in the hall outside his office and tossed his pen onto the paperwork scattered across his desk. He looked up as Rick DeShields gingerly levered himself into the office chair. His friend's broad smile faded with the effort.

"Still hurting?" Chris said. He wore round wire frames and a quarter zip with a Farmer's Brew Pub logo.

Rick rubbed the pain from his knee. "Getting better, but please, let's not re-arrange the entire bookshop again anytime soon."

Chris furrowed his brows in sympathy. "Couldn't have done it without you."

"That's what friends are for." Rick grinned. "Feel free to abuse me again. Anytime."

Chris laughed shortly. "I just hope it was worth it."

Rick looked around the small and dim office. "Dude, it's spring out there. Why are you inside?"

"These guys want to buy the bookshop." Chris held up an envelope from BazillionBooks. "I could take their offer, then I'd have plenty of time to enjoy the weather."

The brew pub owner smiled. "I'm sorry, I thought this was the bookshop office, not the depressing lair of Derrick Downer."

Without thinking, Chris matched his friend's smile. The happy-go-lucky Rick felt it his duty to monitor his attitude. "Not feeling it today."

Rick adjusted himself in the office chair with a sigh. "At least you're still in business, Derrick. Ow."

"Yeah, but—"

"And business will pick up, right? Always has."

"I know, but—"

"Or, I got an idea, you could just take the offer. Take the money and run."

"Advice from rock and roll lyrics." Chris looked away. "Thank you, Steve Miller."

"Don't forget the Silver Bullet Band." Rick leaned forward with a wince. "But I'm serious."

Chris pointed the BazillionBooks envelope at him. "I can't run away, I'm part of the community."

"I knew you'd say that." Rick's smile faded. "What's this community ever done for you?"

"My grandfather built this place, then my dad, now me."

Rick brushed the words away with his hand. "Yeah, yeah, your legacy, I get it. But come on, they're gonna ban books and run you out of here."

Chris barked a laugh. "I'll manage. Somehow."

"That's what you always do: manage, hang on, do the hard thing, never take the easy way." He slumped back in the chair and clamped his jaw shut.

"Don't forget I'm getting a big bag of loot from the rental space." When his friend didn't look up, he added, "Thanks to your help."

"Kennedy Phillips, really?" Rick's eyes narrowed to his. "You're playing the KK card? How much worse can you possibly make it for yourself?"

"The money will buy me a few more months." Rick didn't meet his eyes. "Until it picks back up."

"And this time she'll let you take her to the prom? Are you nuts?"

Chris cocked his head and grinned in reply.

"Wait, I was kidding." His face gaped open. "You actually think you have a chance with her."

Chris tossed the envelope from the big box bookstore aside. "Her money spends like anybody else's."

"She hurt you, man." Rick's voice rose. "All those things you did for her, she just ignored. Like you didn't exist."

"Yet here I am, and there she is." He pointed to himself then to the campaign HQ. "Maybe it's my second chance."

"She was out of your league then and she's out of your league now."

"She's worth fighting for."

"OK." Rick paused a moment. "She's been here for a couple days now, how's it going?"

Chris looked away. "Fine."

"That's not what I hear. Sounds like you two hate each other."

"I'm working through the anger. At least we're

talking." Chris opened his hands. "The rest is gossip. You know how it is."

"I do, and I know how *she* is." Rick waited for his friend to look up. "She broke your heart."

"I'm all healed."

"Wow." Rick's face turned from doubt to awe. "It's not about the money or the store. It's Kennedy."

"It is. And you and I are the only ones who know."

"*She* doesn't know. That's always been the problem." Now his face screwed together in thought. "OK, I can't believe you'd do this, but this time, at least sign the gifts with your name, not 'Secret Admirer,' would you?"

Chris drew his eyes from the rented side back to his friend. "Not my best move, huh?"

"No. She never did find out who sent the flowers, or the cards, or the gummi bears, and then, if I hadn't tackled you, you would have landed a hot air balloon in her back yard." Rick shook his head. "You're a glutton for punishment. A hopeless romantic."

"Inept romantic, I'll buy that, but not hopeless." Chris dropped his voice. "You won't tell anybody."

"I've kept your ineptly romantic secrets for years. I won't blab now."

"I trust you." Chris sighed and looked into the distance. "The hot air balloon was merely the method; it was really all about the rose. I was going to give her one long-stemmed red rose."

Rick's hands rose in surrender. "No, you're hopeless. Totally."

Chapter 7

Kennedy unlocked her side of the store front and turned on the lights. According to the text her team would arrive shortly. She had a few minutes to mend a fence. "Knock knock!" She rapped her knuckles on the door frame of the bookstore. "You guys open yet?"

Chloe appeared from the stacks, her hands filled with books. "He's in the back." She gestured with her chin.

Kennedy introduced herself and threaded her way through the bookcases to the tiny office. Chris leaned back in the green leather office chair and raised an eyelid.

"I came to give you the rent." She dropped an envelope onto the desk. "And to apologize."

"Thank you." He felt his shoulders relax. "Apologize for what?"

"For lying."

"Lying?"

"Well not really lying." Kennedy didn't know what to do with her hands. "This is hard for me."

"I'll bet." He pointed to the small chair. "Must be the first time you've ever been wrong."

"That's harsh," she said and sat down. "But probably true."

Chris hadn't expected that response. "What is this about?"

"Biology lab. I wasn't your lab partner."

"Duh."

"You knew and you went along with it?"

Chris held up a hand. "You started it."

"No, you brought it up. You said we were lab partners, sophomore year, that's what you said."

"I didn't." Chris grinned. "And yet here *you* are apologizing."

"But—" Kennedy clenched her jaw tightly. All I wanted to do was clear the air, and he's laughing at me.

"You people never knew I existed," Chris said. "I was a nobody; you were one of the cool kids."

"You people—"

"It's my turn." He stood up behind the desk. "Of course we weren't lab partners, I was in AP Bio and you took Fun With Test Tubes."

She popped to her feet. "I got an A in that class."

"A petri dish could get an A in that class."

"I didn't come in here to be insulted." She turned to leave.

"Maybe not, but you came in here to my office." He came around the desk. "You always took the easy classes, Kennedy. You had to keep up your grade point average. To please your Daddy."

"I graduated tenth in the class," she snapped. "You?"

"Lower, that's true, but I got into a good college. You?"

Kennedy spun away from him. Nearly blind with

anger and embarrassment, she somehow managed to escape the warren of books. Chris couldn't help but smile as he sat back down.

"That went well." Chloe slipped into the office and settled into the chair.

"You heard?"

"Hard not to." She pulled a tuft of hair behind her ear. The rings on her fingers sparkled in the dim office light. "I sense you know each other."

"Same high school, different planet."

"I get it. Cliques." She nodded. "We still have those at good old BCHS. They think I'm a jock."

"Because you play softball."

"Yeah, that's my pigeonhole." Chloe waved her black fingernails. "That's all they see."

"But you're in plays and you sing, right?"

"Nobody knows that, 'cause I'm work/study in the afternoons. Only in school in the morning."

Chris grinned at his only employee. "Yeah, well I think you're well-rounded. When I was in high school, we only had two cliques: The rich and famous, and the AYO's."

Chloe arched an eyebrow and the tiny jewel followed.

"All You Others."

She settled her hands in her lap and leaned forward. "And how did that make you feel?"

Chris laughed at the serious look on her face. "Well, I don't know, out of it, not cool, invisible."

The teenager nodded her head toward the empty half of the building. "Yet here she is. Your guest."

Chris slumped deeper into the big green leather chair. "I need her money." His eyes drifted away. "I wish I didn't."

"She needs your store front, Uncle." When his eyes didn't return, she said, "She is kinda cute, in a Barbie kinda way."

"Don't even start." His eyes snapped to hers. "No, you I need. Not her."

"Just saying." Chloe stood up.

Chris pointed to the door. "Out now. Back to work."

Chloe raised her hands in mock defeat. "Oh, I forgot to tell you. That guy with the sign is marching around in front of the store again.

It would be a cold day in hell if he were interested in Queen Kennedy, Chris thought as he stood up. "Thanks, I'll send him on his way." A very cold day.

Kennedy fumed as she burst from the bookstore into her rented space. She barely managed to keep from running. The last thing she wanted was to give that creep the satisfaction of chasing her away. So, good, she didn't run away.

But the nerve of that man. I'm paying him rent money to be here, and I go over there to apologize and what? I end up leaving? I wasn't the guilty party, he was, and he practically threw me out? Just who does he think he is?

She probably would have continued in this vein, but her phone bleeped, and she looked through the window to see the Rassmussen truck double parked. She ran outside to remove the traffic cones. In the hectic unpacking, she filed away her thoughts of Chris Lennox.

Chapter 8

"You're gonna fall off that ladder and kill yourself, Ms. Phillips. Be careful!"

"Just hold on to your end, Alvin, I'm fine." The ladder wobbled, but Kennedy grabbed hold of the window molding and it settled. She managed to seat the davit over one nail, then another, and held her hands away. "Ta da!"

At the far end of the banner Alvin shook his head as a grin escaped. "Thought I was gonna lose you."

"No worries, I'm fine, and the sign looks great." She scampered down the ladder and joined him beneath it.

"Rassmussen for Senate," the young man read. "Does look good, but was it worth the risk?"

Kennedy punched him playfully in the shoulder. "No pain, no gain."

"Why you make the big money." He folded up one of the stepladders. "What's next?"

Kennedy led him into the chaos that was the campaign headquarters. Staffers were hanging posters and unpacking boxes of literature, while manning the phones signing up volunteers. It was loud, and to Kennedy it was wonderful. All those people were working together under her leadership.

"Help those kids with the Senator's picture." She gestured to two girls trying to center the large color print in the front window. "I'll bring the other ladder inside."

At the door, Kennedy stopped a staffer pinning another Rassmussen pin onto her coat. "Cheryl? It's Cheryl, right?"

The girl blushed. "Yes, Ma'am."

"I don't think you need seven pins, do you?"

"But I love the Senator so much!"

"I do too, but we need to pass them out to voters."

As Cheryl unpinned several of the round metal pins, Kennedy whispered in her ear. "Keep a couple for yourself, but make sure all your friends get one too, OK?" The girl grinned and Kennedy stepped onto the sidewalk and picked up the other stepladder.

"They got you doing manual labor?" Gena Cobb said. "I thought you were in management."

Kennedy set the ladder down and looked at the other woman. Short hair a little out of style, stern features, forty-ish. "See? A good leader and dirty hands?"

Sammi pushed between them and giggled. "You go, girl!"

Gena grimaced. "Speaking of which, is your leader going to be here tonight?"

"Of course he is, right KK? He wouldn't miss the grand opening of his campaign headquarters."

"Of course he wouldn't, Sammi," she said as she picked up the ladder. "I'll see you guys tonight?"

"Wouldn't miss it," Gena said. "It's a big deal for Benton Center." Next to her, Sammi's smile was deeper and more friendly.

While she worked her way into the HQ with the

ladder, Kennedy realized that Scott hadn't called her today.

On the other side of the partition in the Lennox Family Bookstore it was loud. Not busy, empty in fact, no customers, but loud from the activity next door. More coming and going the last couple of days than he'd had the previous month. Chris tapped the pad on his grandfather's desk with his index finger.

A trumpet blared through the thin wall. He flinched, and leapt to his feet. She's scaring away customers. First the weirdo with the sign, now a marching band. He ran to the door but couldn't open it for the throng of people. Not customers, not book lovers, people, a mob of them, trying to enter the campaign headquarters. His tripod sign had been flattened onto the sidewalk. He forced the door open and returned it to its place.

The trumpet blasted again, along with a trombone and a snare drum. A couple of cheerleaders bounced to the music and waved pom-poms. He snarled his way through them and fought his way into the store front.

Kennedy appeared out of the crowd in front of him. "Isn't it great?"

"No, it's not." He struggled against the press of people to remain in front of her. "It's killing my business."

"Great for business," she said. "Bet you haven't seen this many people in years."

He stepped aside to avoid a kid carrying an enormous box on his shoulder. "Yes, but no, that's not what I mean, it's bad for *my* business."

"All these people, all this excitement." She turned away and signed a document on a clipboard. "Thanks, hon." To Chris she said, "Confirmation from NBC News."

"But you said the opening was tonight, not now."

"It is. We open in a couple of hours," Kennedy beamed. "They're all here to practice. To get ready for the Senator's arrival. We want everything to go perfectly."

"But people can't get through my door. They can't even *see* my door."

Kennedy frowned, brightened, then jammed her phone to her ear. "It's Scott!"

Chris watched her cradle the phone with her shoulder and turn away into the crowd. He sighed. I know she's paying me rent, but this is ridiculous. He fought his way out the door, through the musicians and into the relative quiet of his bookstore. Great, it's quieter. Great, no customers.

Chapter 9

Kennedy stared at the bits of confetti on the floor of the darkened HQ. Some of the balloons bounced jauntily, several drooped wearily as if mimicking her mood. The worst was the clump of empty microphone stands.

She had been proud of her preparations for the Grand Opening of the campaign in Benton Center, the staff, the phone bank, the signs, the banners, the literature, all set and ready to inspire votes for Scott. She was proudest of her liaison efforts with the press. The carefully worded releases, the planned interviews and photo ops, and the NBC camera crew feeding live updates to the Cleveland and Columbus markets. All her hard work leading up to tonight.

And the candidate himself hadn't shown up.

"Big donor meeting tonight in Westerville," he'd said on their Facetime. "Guy's loaded, KK, very interested in what I can do for him. And the state. I'd be a fool to miss this."

"But all the people—"

"You can handle it, can't you?"

"Sure, but they—"

"You're my voice, my star. You know what I'd tell them." She imagined him grinning through the phone. "Hell, you wrote most of my speech anyway."

"Yes, but they want to see *you*."

"They'll see me soon enough. Just re-schedule for the weekend."

"The Country Club meet is this weekend."

"With your dad, right." Scott's words ran together. "Don't worry, I won't miss *that*."

"I don't think I can get everybody back here tomorrow. Especially the press. They weren't happy—"

"Do you want me to send Brenda?"

That had stung the worst. Brenda, his personal assistant. She'd bristled, "I don't need her help, I need you here, Scott."

She imagined him doing the balancing thing with his hands. "Lots of money, which we need, and the press which we need. Balance it out."

"And tell them what time you'll be here? Will they believe me?"

"It's their job, of course they'll believe you. They need a story."

"Darn it, Scott, it took everything I had to keep them from running tape of me at the microphone and not you."

"And I love you for it, Sweetie." He laughed. "You're the best. Shoot, you're the only one who could pull it off."

There had been more, but that was the jist. She was so valuable to him that she could rearrange everything. She could take the hit, and smooth it all out so he could just glide on through. Like he always did.

And she had. She'd stepped to the mic and told the overflow crowd that Scott "was on a secret mission" to improve the lives of Conway County. The Senator was super sorry for not being able to attend but would try his best to arrive tomorrow afternoon. She'd been proud of keeping her cool and not crying, and a little scared that it had been so easy for her to lie in front of so many people.

She had summarized Scott's platform, the band had played, yard signs and buttons were distributed, the wine and cheese consumed. She'd made the best of a bad situation, but that had not been good enough for everyone.

Sammi had been disappointed. Supportive, but saddened. Maggie, too, but her eyes gleamed brightly, unlike Sammi's.

Teddi took the high road. "You did what you could. Get them next time." A bag of baked goods and a warm hug sealed the deal.

Gena had tried to hide her glee, but not very hard. She had muttered things like "comeuppance" and "serves her right" to Connie. The pinch-faced lady added, "Who does she think she is?" Kennedy had worked so hard to convince the Gossip Club that she could organize a proper campaign launch, but had stood in front of them, defeated.

Her Dad had been there, too. They hadn't spoken, but she knew what he thought. "My daughter can't do anything right. Thinks she's a mover and shaker but can't even do this." He'd stood alone in the back of the room and left without saying anything to her. Now she'd have to face his disappointment at the Country Club.

Chris snapped the lid of his laptop shut. Nearly nothing to show for a whole day. Even Chloe's bubbly personality had failed to improve his mood. He glanced at the letter from

BazillionBooks still lying on his desk. Soon to be his only choice.

But what had he expected with the chaos going on all day next door? He'd held back his anger and waited till the noise subsided before trying to speak to her again. Now he strode out of the bookstore into the campaign office.

Two steps inside the door Chris jerked to a halt. Kennedy was slumped like a rag doll, her head lolling on a table, her arms limp. Serves her right, he began, but stopped. He'd never seen her like this: clothes not perfect, hair a rat's nest, obviously exhausted. And defeated. He'd always seen her as a winner. She was the queen of BCHS. He didn't understand what had happened to her, but exited silently, and carefully shut the door behind him.

Chapter 10

Chris was rarely brave enough to venture into the Pot & Flagon when the Gossip Club was in session but decided to give it a try the next morning. He took a deep breath and pulled open the door. Keeping his eyes strictly on the counter, not the table in the front window, he ordered a cranberry scone and a latte. Only after the waitress slid them across the counter, did he venture a glance at the ladies.

Gena was holding court, jabbing a finger around the table to emphasize her points. Teddi held her hands in her lap and watched. Sammi carefully set down her coffee mug and whispered something to Maggie. Mary Jane, several others, and the lady with the pinched face—he thought her name was Morse—kept their eyes on the speaker.

Chris was heading for a small table next to the brick wall, when Gena raised her voice. "Why don't we ask Mr. Lennox? He was there."

He continued toward the open table, hoping they

weren't really talking about him. Sammi called, "Chris? We have an empty spot. Would you like to join us?"

Caught in the open with no place to hide, Chris reluctantly sat down between her and another woman he recognized but didn't know.

"What do you think?" Gena demanded. "You heard it all."

Chris hid his face behind the heavy ceramic mug. "Heard what?"

"The screw-up. The chaos. The big botch." Gena plumbed the table for affirmation. Many of the ladies bobbed their heads and focused their gaze on him.

Chris took a bite of the scone, and it stuck in his throat. "I assume you're talking about the event last night at the campaign HQ."

"What else happened lately in Ben Cen?" Gena demanded.

"We deserve to know," Mary Jane said. Sammi nudged Chris with her elbow.

"Kennedy and I don't share a lot, as you all know." He set down the mug and looked around the table. "We've never traveled in the same social circle."

Gena waved away his comment. "But the guest of honor never showed up. How can you have an event without the main attraction?"

"Who is kinda cute, I think," Mary Jane looked to Gena.

"Whatever." Gena refrained from returning her look. "She came waltzing in here fresh from her jog saying how organized she was and how she could handle the responsibility. She blew it."

"That's unfair." Sammi's voice cracked as she leaned forward. "She's been putting in a lot of hours. Working her tail off."

Chris watched her fold her arms across her chest and returned the nudge. "From what I gather, it wasn't her fault Rassmussen didn't show."

"She's in charge of the event and didn't know?" Gena nodded around the table. "Why did she even send out invitations?"

"Well, I heard—"

"That's not what—"

"Give the man time to speak," Teddi said softly.

Chris nodded a thank you to the barista. "I was going over there to complain about the noise when she got the call. An hour before. A little less." He looked at the foam on his latte. "The camera crew was already setting up. I guess she couldn't cancel. I was right next to her."

"Serves her right." The woman he didn't know bore her gaze into him.

"That was my first thought, too. Things have always gone her way." Chris shook his head. "Someone has always been around to bail her out." He paused. "This time?"

"I don't think it was her fault." Sammi spoke more confidently now. "She didn't do anything to deserve being screwed over by her boss. She did the best she could."

"But—"

Chris held up his hand. "I'm not here to defend Kennedy. She can do that herself." He stared at the pairs of eyes around the table. "What I really came here for today is an update on the book banning. Ms. Kimble, is there any news?"

The second-grade teacher smiled. "Thanks for asking. Just the Board of Education meeting next week."

"You might want to go, Chris." Teddi nodded her head.

"He doesn't have any kids. Why should he go?" Gena looked at Teddi, not Chris.

"I'm trying to sell books. I should know what's going on in town."

Gena transferred her gaze from Teddi to Chris. "Yes, you should." Her voice sounded like it had been her idea all along.

Thankfully his mug was empty, and his plate held only crumbs. "I'd better get going. I have an event to organize myself."

He felt their eyes as he got to his feet. "Story hour. First time in the smaller space."

"Hope it works out for you." Sammi pecked him on the cheek. Chris could feel her baby bump.

"It isn't Dr. Seuss, is it?" Gena raised her eyebrows. "I hear he's a no-no."

"No, Maurice Sendak. *Where the Wild Things Are.* Who could be against that?"

"A great book," Joanie said. "One of my favorites."

After Chris left and the bell tinkled, Gena said, "Apparently a lot of people." Around the table they copied her attitude and nodded thoughtfully.

Chris nearly ran into Kennedy as he reached the door of the bookstore. After sharing an awkward series of "oops," "my fault," "no, my fault," he said, "You can't be on your way to the Pot & Flagon."

Determination replaced embarrassment on her face. "I have to."

"But they're in there. All of them."

Kennedy's face pulled together like a string in a cloth bag. "Why do you care?"

"I don't like getting grilled—"

"So you think I can't handle it?" She jammed both fists on her waist.

"No, not what I—"

"I've been dealing with them for years, you haven't."

Chris stepped back and held up his palms in surrender. "Of course you can, but why put yourself in that position?"

Kennedy nodded as if she agreed. "You were there, right, so you know all about me? Sure. Like everybody around here does."

"Hey, if you want your fair share of abuse, go right ahead. Don't say I didn't warn you." Before she could respond, he spun on his heel and retreated to his bookstore.

Kennedy took one step to follow, stopped suddenly, and threw out her arms in exasperation. "Why is everybody always telling me what to do?" She whirled around and marched off toward the Pot & Flagon.

Chapter 11

Kennedy continued muttering to herself as she stomped her way to the Pot & Flagon. Her father telling her what to do, Gena and Teddi and the others telling her what to do, and now the guy she's renting office space from, her *landlord*, thinks he can tell me what to do. Who's next, she asked herself as she ripped the door open so violently that the bell didn't tinkle.

Who's next himself was seated at the table in the front window. He was surrounded by the Ladies Gossip Club, a group of women Kennedy barely recognized as all their eyes were focused on him, and all their mouths were closed.

"Scott," she cried out loud and ran to the table.

The senator was confused for an instant as he turned, and she grabbed him in a hug as he struggled to his feet. They stood there several seconds before one of the ladies muttered, "Get a room."

Kennedy didn't care as they stepped out of the

embrace, but then it hit her. "When did you get in?"

"Just a few minutes ago. I was just stopping in to get you a coffee and the ladies here——" He paused to flash them a smile. "They waylaid me."

Kennedy looked from his blue eyes to the eight other pairs watching rabidly from the table. "You didn't tell me you were coming."

"Knew you were busy." Scott flashed his brilliant smile at her. "Surprise!" He leaned in to kiss her, but she stepped back.

"You should have told me." She grabbed his hand and turned to face Gena and the ladies. "Thanks for taking care of him for me. I've got him now."

He resisted her tug. "Pull up a chair and sit down."

Sammi clapped her hands excitedly. "It's not every day we get a real celebrity. And the senator bought you a latte, just how you like it." She pointed to the to-go cup on the table.

The other ladies agreed, Scott smiled encouragingly, Gena watched as if keeping notes, and Kennedy settled in front of her latte. "Still hot," she said. "Thank you."

"So then, Senator Rassmussen." Gena spoke into the few seconds of quiet at the table. "Since we didn't get a chance to hear you last night at the Grand Opening." Gena paused to make sure she was being heard. "I'm assuming you have another whatever you call it, presser, scheduled for tonight." Her tone indicated a mashup of question, declaration and suggestion.

Scott cleared his throat and turned to Kennedy with raised eyebrows. "I haven't scheduled anything for today."

His gaze hardened as she continued. "I didn't know when you were getting into town. Senator."

Gena nodded around the table to make sure they

noticed. Kennedy could feel it.

Scott covered his face in a smile. "No, of course, you didn't. I'll get Brenda on it."

It seemed very quiet to Kennedy. Inside the Pot & Flagon no one spoke. Outside in the Square people were frozen into place. Her mind raced, but she managed not to blush. "Or," she said clearly, "we could hold off until the event at the Country Club this weekend. I've issued a dozen sets of press credentials for that."

"That might work." Scott placed his hands on the table and slid back his chair. Kennedy held her cup with both hands.

"Wait, if you can, senator." Gena made sure she faced him and didn't face Kennedy. "Since we aren't going to hear from you today officially, perhaps you could help us with a local issue?"

Rassmussen grinned. "Of course."

Gena gestured to Joanie Kimble. The second-grade teacher looked from her to the handsome politician. "I wonder if you have a position on book banning? It's becoming an issue here in Benton Center."

He laughed. "I was hoping for a serious issue like which cream cheese I use on my bagels." The women laughed warily. He glanced at Kennedy and the women shifted their eyes to her.

Kennedy returned Scott's gaze. She had done the research on the issue weeks ago, but he had never stated his position. When he didn't speak, she said, "Sharpening our position on that is one of our goals the next week or so. We're working on it." She felt him clasp her hand beneath the table.

"Can we get back to you on this?" he said.

Gena's brows knotted together, and Joanie said, "Sure, of course. It's just that there's a big Board of

Education meeting coming up, and, you know."

Rassmussen nodded his head toward Kennedy. "We'll get it out to you before then. For sure." He cleared his chair and stood up.

Kennedy took his hand, they made their goodbyes, and she led him outside. "You saved my life in there," he said quietly.

"You threw me under the bus in there." She continued walking, nearly pulling him across the street into the Square. Reaching an isolated bench, she pointed and he sat down.

"Sorry?" Scott made his innocent little boy face, and she almost giggled.

"What did you do to be sorry for?"

A thought struck him. "Got a big check from a rich donor?"

"That's nice, but you made me look like a fool."

The candidate looked confused. "Those ladies think you're a fool? No way. They're nice."

"They're snakes, dear, most all of them."

"Maybe to you, but I charmed them. They love me." He mimicked fingering a musical tube and charming a snake from a wicker basket. "Da da da, da da."

"Cute," she said and dropped to the bench beside him. "They're vipers who think I'm an incompetent nobody."

Scott held his hands apart and stopped humming. "Cat fight. I'm *not* involved, not gonna *be* involved."

Kennedy sighed. "It isn't your fight, it's mine. But you know, I gave you all that background on book banning in January."

He took her hand. "I made you look bad, huh. OK, when we release our position, I'll make sure you get the credit."

She stood up and he followed. "Best we can do now."

He smiled as if releasing a weight. "Now then, about the accommodations. I can stay out by the interstate if you wish. Brenda got a block of rooms for the staff. Saved a bunch of money."

Kennedy led him down a slanted path to the corner. "No, I told you we have rooms, two rooms, in this cute little BNB."

"You told me?"

"You probably didn't read your emails."

"Me? I always read my e-mails."

"Sure you do, Scott, sure you do." She grinned weakly and led him across the street.

Chapter 12

From the floor in the front window of the Lennox Family Bookshop, Chris watched Kennedy drag a tall, good-looking man to a bench in the Square and practically force him to sit down. He didn't know why she seemed to always be in his line of sight. It's not that he was looking for her, he was hoping some more people would show up for his little kids reading club.

As he looked closer, something in her bearing didn't seem to fit. The man on the bench, maybe Rassmussen, was laughing, and she stood somewhat apart, rigid as a statue. Someone was approaching the store, and he craned his neck to see.

He had managed to save some space at the front of the crowded store for one of his favorite activities. A soft, brightly colored, ribbed rug defined the space. Throw pillows and stuffed animals waited on it, and usually four or five mothers and their kids inhabited it. Today only two moms and three kids. He looked hopefully at the door.

"We'll get started in a minute," he said as he climbed to his feet. "Just want to see who's at the door."

One of the kids raised his arms in menacing claws. "Grrrrr!"

"You're getting into character, Marcus, hold that thought. I'll be right back."

Instead of coming in, a figure was standing in front of the bookshop door. Chris held it open. "Come on in."

"Not coming in. Won't come in." The man wore a rumpled, dark suit, white collared shirt, and a red necktie. He held a placard on a wooden stick.

"It's a great book today, Mr. Morse."

"It's the work of the devil, sir."

"No, it's about the joys of being a kid." Chris kept a smile on his face. "Come on in and listen."

"I shall not."

"They enjoy pretending, Mr. Morse. It's all about imagination."

"It's about children turning into monsters. There's no such thing."

"No, but they turn back into kids at the end. Come on, just watch how much they enjoy it."

"Your books are grooming these precious children into unholy abominations." Morse held the sign in front of himself like a shield and began to march across the storefront. "Save Our Children" it read.

"Just don't block the door, if you please." Chris keyed the Benton Center PD into his cell. They would lead the man away as they had the other times.

"Mrs. Turner, you don't have to go. We'll get started right away." Chris stopped in the doorway.

"He's scared, we have to go." She twisted to keep hold of her child's hand.

Chris squatted down in front of Marcus. "But you're

a big scary monster. You're a wild thing."

The little boy ran his arm across his snotty nose. "I'm scared."

"No, he's scared. That guy out there is scared of monsters."

Marcus narrowed his eyes.

"You think if you roar, you can scare him away? If you gave him a great big roar?"

Marcus shook his head, no, and backed into the safety of his mother's long skirt.

"What if I helped?"

Marcus shook his head no.

"And if your mom roared, too?"

Another shake.

"And if the other kids roared? If all of us roared together? A big, gigantic, terrifying monster roar? What do you think?"

Marcus looked around doubtfully as the other mom and her two little ones huddled together in front of the window.

Chris peeked through the glass to see the PD cruiser pull to a stop. "OK, everybody," he whispered. "When I count to three, we all yell our best monster roar. Ready?"

He held the door open. "One, two, and three!"

Morse looked over his shoulder at the sound from the bookshop and flinched. The officers led him to the squad car and placed him in the back seat. One of them nodded to Chris.

"Way to go, everybody. That guy says books are bad, but we know they aren't right?"

The kids cheered and ran back to their places on the reading rug. Mrs. Turner said, "That man scares me, Mr. Lennox. I don't know if we can come back next time."

"Then let's make sure we enjoy this time," Chris

said with a smile. He followed her back into the shop and plopped down on the rug among the kids. "So who wants to read first?"

Mrs. Turner nodded a smile at the other mom and joined the chaos on the floor.

An hour later, Chloe dropped into the office chair. For several seconds Chris didn't speak or seemingly notice her arrival.

"Uh, hello."

He rotated the green leather chair. "You're on time. A good quality in an employee."

"Yeah, your only employee."

"My best employee."

"Cuz you can't afford another one."

Chris straightened up. "If I could, I would find one with a little nicer attitude."

"Is it my attitude or the bottom line that's the problem here?"

"Or me talking out my problems with a sixteen-year-old."

"A precocious sixteen-year-old hitting .387 and playing an MVP shortstop." Chloe opened her hands as if accepting the MVP award.

Chris laughed. "You know, I always feel better talking to you. I must be losing it."

Chloe settled in her chair and put on her grown-up, serious face. "What's the probs?"

"You know what it is, we don't have enough people buying books."

"Like duh, nobody reads."

"Which we both know and are going to ignore." He squinted at her. "What can I, well, the two of us, do to get more people in here?"

"Be popular."

"Channeling *Wicked*, are we? I'm gonna be pop-U-lar?" He had to wave his hands to stop her from singing, "I'm serious."

"Got an idea, boss. The team, the softball team, needs to find a bonding activity. Coach wants us to do some kind of public service."

Chris nodded. "Uh-huh."

"I'm thinking our obligation could be your salvation."

"I'm lost." Chris asked himself again why he was talking business with a teenager.

"We got to put in some hours, and you need a dose of popularity. So."

"So?"

"So we, the team, take over your story hour thingy. We read to the kids. They find us wildly popular, the moms buy more books, I get an enormous raise and you stay in business. Maybe even expand back to the full store."

"Little girls would love it."

"Little boys too. Most of us babysit on the weekends. We must know dozens of little kids by name. Can't miss." Chloe stood and gave him a two-finger salute. "My job here is done."

"No, you just came on shift. But thank you, it's a good idea."

She waved a lanky arm over her head and disappeared into the cramped aisle of books.

That's why, Chris said to himself. That's why I talk to teenagers.

Chapter 13

"*What exactly is* a flagon?" Scott swirled the red wine in his stemmed glass hoping to find the answer in its depth.

Across the small table from him Kennedy stifled a smile. "You're kidding, right?"

"Never heard of it." He took a sip of the wine.

She set down her glass. "It's like a carafe, but smaller."

He looked at her blankly. "You're killing me, KK."

She sighed. How could anyone be so smart in some things and thick as a brick in others? "It's a jug. Like on the metal sign outside?"

Scott glubbed down the rest of the glass and slapped his hand on the table between them. "Why can't they use words that everyone understands?" He looked around as the guitar player tuned his strings and plunked the mic. "But I have to admit, this is a pretty nice place to have a drink and hear some music."

"Venue," she said in a whisper. "Not a place." When he opened his mouth to speak, she held a finger across her lips. As the twelve-string guitar melded with the singer's throaty baritone, she looked around the wine bar. The original brick walls and racks of wine bottles caught the subtle pools of track light to transform the 19th century grocery store into a warm and intimate performing space. The Coffee Pot in front during the day, and the Wine Flagon in the rear in the evenings. It was a terrific use of the old building. She nodded as she took in the ambience.

"This song sounds familiar." Scott furrowed his brow in contemplation. When Kennedy didn't answer quickly, he said, "Need a little help here."

She often told herself she was indispensable to his political campaign but didn't know that extended into musicology. "That's Terry McGrath." She laid it out there hoping the clue would be enough for him, but she didn't want him to fail. "Terry and the Love Pirates?"

"Yes! That's what I thought." He reached for her hand and squeezed it. "How could I manage without you?"

She returned the squeeze with a smile. You can't, she thought.

At the end of McGrath's set, he led them back to the BNB. "Tell me again why we have to have separate rooms?"

She pecked him on the cheek. "You know why. The walls have eyes."

"You mean the wallpaper in my room? Those pink blobs look like cabbages."

She wasn't sure he was making a joke but laughed anyway. "Oh, hey, about the presser. You want me to set something up for tomorrow, before the Country Club event?"

He stopped on the narrow, stone staircase of the BNB. "Could you? I thought we blew it today."

"We kinda did, but I can reach out to the locals. If not, we'll do it at the donor event."

"No, now that I think about it, let's wait till we can

set it up for the big markets. Maybe do both?" He took another step up and turned to her. "You know, Kennedy, I'd be lost without you."

She slapped his arm playfully. "You'd manage somehow."

He reached down to her at the bottom of the steps. "Aren't you coming up? I promise to be good."

"Got a date," she grinned. "With my dad."

"Good, I'm beat anyway." He held the door open and waved as she drove away. Moments later in his room, he spoke into his cell. "Brenda? It's me . . . yes . . . for sure."

Grantham Phillips handed his daughter a glass of pinot noir. "How's our boy doing?" He sat down on the love seat opposite her. Behind him a fire crackled comfortably under the heavy wood mantel piece.

Kennedy smiled. "He's *our* boy now? That means you're writing him a big check?"

"Those are questions of your own, dear, not an answer to mine."

She read his face. "OK. Not great, he botched the opening, but on the right track. Overall."

"He's still middle of the road, isn't he?"

"In this state, the middle is a tough place to be." She sipped her wine and kept her eyes on her father's.

"Absolutely, Kennedy. You're on the ball."

She warmed at his praise. "Yeah, so the hard part is, taking a legitimate stand that's not extreme, but at the same time meaningful."

"Well said. You've been putting your time in Columbus to good use." He tipped his scotch tumbler and the cubes jingled.

"Thank you, Daddy, that means a lot."

He pointed his empty glass at a file folder on the coffee table between them. "Do you want to take a look?"

Kennedy read the tab: *Rassmussen, Scott W.* "You didn't. Tell me you didn't have him investigated."

"Of course I did." From the bar he said, "It's basic research, not an investigation."

Kennedy had to bite her tongue not to scream. "You said you would let me handle this."

Grantham settled onto the sofa. "More wine?"

Kennedy tried to slow down her speech and failed. "I don't want wine, I want to know what you're doing."

Her father spoke slowly. "I'm doing what I would do if I were in your position."

"You promised not to interfere with the campaign." She could feel her cheeks flush. "You promised to let me do it."

"So go ahead and do it." He sipped his drink and set down the glass. "I'm not interfering."

She jabbed her finger on the folder as her voice increased in pitch. "*This* is interfering."

Infuriatingly, he smiled at her. "Only if you look at it."

"What?" she nearly screamed. "We had an understanding." Her eyes glared. "A deal."

"We still do." He nearly shrugged. "Depends on what you do with the information in this folder."

She forced herself to relax. "What do you mean?"

"Do you want to take a look at it? See what my people found or not?"

"No. No, I do not want to see it." She defied him to contradict her. "I want to figure it out for myself."

Her father reached his drink across the table and tapped her glass with it. "That's the right answer."

She clamped her lips together. You let me think I'm in charge, but you still hold the leash. She carefully placed her glass next to the file, took a breath. "You were testing me."

"That's a harsh way to put it, Kennedy." He smiled.

"But accurate. You're the only one with the answers. You make all the decisions."

"It is my money." He grinned sheepishly. "And I'm your father."

"Which at this point is irrelevant. I'm managing his county office, and it's important to me."

"I know it is, and it should be." He pointed to the Rassmussen file. "I'm offering you information. If you want to do it on your own, don't use it."

Was this another test? "And you'll release the donation on my say so? Pretty hard to believe."

"Trust me." He raised his eyebrows.

She narrowed her gaze and returned his. "Trust me."

Chapter 14

As Chris walked from his bookshop to the Pot & Flagon, he asked himself again whether his picture would appear if he googled the term "glutton for punishment." What other reason would he have for willfully letting himself be roasted by the Ladies of the Gossip Club?

Pure, unadulterated cussedness, he answered. I will not let them get away with thinking they are the boss of me. He tugged open the tinkly door and strode confidently toward the counter. Until he stumbled over the threshold. He caught himself before hitting the floor but was sure he heard giggling from the front table. He didn't look to see.

"Hazelnut latte, medium, whole milk, Teddi." He kept his eyes on the barista, thankful that she wasn't laughing.

"Haven't seen you in a while, Chris. Have a nice *trip?*" Gena called from behind him.

Teddi set a mug under the steam jet and didn't join the monkey chorus from the table.

He willed his cheeks not to redden. "And one of

your tasty scones, please. Blueberry."

Several minutes later, it seemed closer to an hour as he waited, Teddi slid his breakfast across the counter. He took it and approached the Gossip Club. Halfway to the table he stopped and did a couple of dance steps. "No tripping, just the light fantastic."

"No way." Maggie said with a grin. "A trip."

"Definitely a trip." Sammi added.

"We all saw it, Mr. Lennox, please join us." Gena pointed to an empty seat. "What do you have to say for yourself?"

"I'm a lousy dancer?" That got a few smiles, but no laughter. He tried again. "In what regard?"

Gena's voice was as stern as a Western Reserve Puritan. "As the owner of the only bookshop in Benton Center."

The others looked up from their pastries. "Business is slow."

They watched him but remained silent.

"Small business in general. The Buy Local messaging is not enough. No one reads. Video games. Screen time. The lack of attention span. The controversy."

"That last bit is interesting. The rest is the same old story, Chris." Mary Jane leaned closer. "What do you think that's about? The controversy."

"They only read to support their own ideas. They don't enjoy reading. They use books to attack others' opinions."

"That's awful." Sammi held her hands on her baby bump. "I love reading. I hope my baby will."

Chris tore a bite off his scone. "I do too, but in schools reading is being taught for the utilitarianism of it: how to read labels, compare prices, make wise purchases. But pleasure, no."

Maggie gestured with her mug. "And to pass the state tests. Don't forget that." Chris nodded in agreement.

"Schools need to educate consumers. We want educated consumers, don't we?" Gena's voice had an edge, Chris' didn't. "You can get a scanner to 'read' a bar code."

"That's pretty cynical," Sammi said. "Where's the fun?"

"Can't teach fun. That's controversial." Chris looked them each in the eye.

"Joanie said something very similar in here last week." Mary Jane nodded. "A Yelp review is cut and dried. Literature is not."

"Different ideas and opinions."

Chris bobbed his head. "Yeah, so it's easier and less controversial to teach reading for straight comprehension, than for enjoyment or critical thinking."

"Egads, not that!"

"Yup, fill in the multiple-choice bubbles on the answer sheet, don't bother with the essay."

Gena glared at the faces around the table. "We're getting a little ahead of ourselves. Joanie teaches second grade."

"That's where it starts." This from the pinch-faced woman. Chris had never realized how much she resembled her husband, Mr. Morse. "It should start at home."

Gena hushed her with a glance. "But that's not why we called you over, Mr. Lennox."

"I was summoned? I didn't know."

"Be that as it may, we have several questions." Gena checked a notebook in her hand. "You told us about your business, so we need to ask how you intend to solve this dearth of book buying?"

"Uh, I hope you all stop by and pick up some books."

Gena sniffed. "Question three, after the campaign

will you get your office space back?"

Chris drank some latte. This was what he had been expecting. "They have a three-month lease and can extend to six. Let's see what happens."

"Speaking of which, how is the Rassmussen campaign going? It doesn't look so good from here."

"Kennedy is putting in a lot of time, I have to admit. Her staff seems small, and the candidate didn't do her any favors." Chris shook his head. "I don't know. She's not my problem."

"Ladies?" Gena looked around the table. "Teddi?" The barista shook her head.

"OK, then." Gena lowered her voice and the faces around the table leaned in. "We are counting on you, Mr. Lennox. You're our spy."

"Pardon me?"

"We're counting on you to keep us informed. We need to know exactly how the campaign is going, and—" She dropped her voice to whisper. "—how well Ms. Kennedy is doing her job." She nodded. "There is great interest in her around town."

Interrogation is one thing, he thought, but not espionage. He stood up. "Thank you for your time this morning, ladies. It's been interesting to say the least."

At the door he heard hushed voices behind him. One said, "See, I told you." Another said, "Typical male."

Chris was still grinning as he passed the Rassmussen HQ and entered his bookshop. He had stood up to them.

Chapter 15

Kennedy watched Chris pass her window and heard him struggle with the door. When it finally banged open, she managed to re-focus on what the woman was saying.

"—I guess what I'm saying is, it's too cozy. Cozy, you know, small town, homey, and well, little." She brought her fingertips together and aimed her smile at Scott.

He nodded and smiled, but Kennedy knew he had no idea what she was talking about. Tossing him a quick glance, she focused on the other woman.

Brenda Venditti was the manager of the Rassmussen For Senate campaign. Short, like a pixie, cute leaning toward cutesy, perky and bubbly. Well-dressed, tending to overdressed, with a two-tone voice: husky for talking to men, and higher pitched for women. A wannabe, her father would label her: All sizzle and no meat.

She was already the campaign manager when Kennedy was named the county director, and they were stuck with each other. Now Brenda was trying to convince

Scott that her selection of the campaign headquarters was wrong, and that Benton Center itself was the wrong place as well.

"But think of it like this." Brenda's dark eyes flashed around the office before returning to Scott's. "What are we trying to say about our campaign? What image are we trying to establish?"

Scott stared blankly at her.

"I mean." She leaned closer to him and dropped the tenor of her voice. "How are we messaging our identity?"

Scott looked pleasantly confused.

Kennedy grinned. "Indeed."

"Are we little, cozy, long in the tooth? Like this building?" Brenda waited for approval but plunged ahead without it. "Or, are we hip, modern, up to date? Like a new digital spot in the strip mall out by the highway?"

Scott nodded noncommittedly.

"That's what we want, isn't it?" Brenda looked to Kennedy. "Relevancy, right?"

Kennedy held her gaze before saying, "I take it you're not happy with the office space."

Brenda slumped and waved a limp arm. "Is this who we are? Who Scott Rassmussen is?"

Kennedy let the line play out a little longer. "Go on."

"Is Scott, is this campaign, all about yesterday or is it about tomorrow?" Brenda focused now on Kennedy. "We are what we appear to be, and this place is, well, shabby."

"Your strategy is to run the campaign according to his image."

Brenda nodded excitedly. "Yes. No door-to-door. No ads in the paper. We go digital, we don't commit to print. We keep our message lean, and light and ready to pivot."

"And our platform?" Kennedy watched her face and

felt the hook set. Her father would be proud.

"Platform? Oh, you mean issue statements." Brenda looked confused, then brightened. "We run on image, not issues."

"What do we stand on? What do we stand for?"

Brenda looked as if she were speaking to a child. "We stand for our image. Words get in the way, and as you know, words alienate people. If we say green, they say yellow, hot, they say cold. That's no way to win an election."

"So, all we do is tell Scott to smile, is that it?"

Brenda clapped her hands. "Exactly!" she patted his knee excitedly. "With his good looks, it's easy."

"I like easy," the candidate said. "I'm good at it."

Kennedy let out a long breath and sat up straighter. She looked from the Square in the front to Alvin and the workers in the middle before settling on the two others in her office. "I'm glad we're getting this out of the way.

"We cannot run a campaign in Benton Center on smoke and mirrors. On image alone." She stared from one to the other. "We need to keep the campaign HQ right where it is and focus on what the people of this district want."

"But—"

"Brenda, you had your turn." Scott looked from one woman to the other.

Kennedy continued, "I'm from this quaint, cozy little town, and I know how it and the whole county operate. For one thing, the average voter turnout in BenCen, the average, is nearly 80 percent. Nearly twice as many people vote here as anywhere else in the state.

"Campaigning on image? Guaranteed failure. Benton Center loves to debate issues. No issues means no engagement, which means no votes. Your method will not work here, Brenda, so we shouldn't go in that direction."

Brenda looked deeply into the candidate's eyes and

said huskily, "Rassy?"

Scott returned her smile and remained silent.

Kennedy straightened the papers on her desk. "That strategy may work in other parts of the state, but not here."

The campaign manager looked one last time at Scott before saying. "You're the local expert, Kennedy. Let's do it your way."

"Great. We need your help." Kennedy clapped her hands and raised her voice. "All right everybody, full staff meeting in five."

Chapter 16

Chris looked at his watch again and shook his head. He'd called the police nearly half an hour ago, and they still hadn't arrived. His first Chloe's Book Club was scheduled to begin soon and the crowd outside the bookshop was growing.

He forced the door open and stepped in front of the man with the picket sign. "Mr. Morse, a word?"

"Mr. Lennox. I know my rights."

Chris forced a smile. "As I know mine."

The half-dozen protesters stopped marching and gathered around the two. They chanted "Ban the books" several times before Morse signaled them to stop. "Is there a problem?"

Morse didn't appear to be high, and Chris could smell no alcohol on his breath, so he assumed it was a legitimate question. "Well, for one thing, customers can't get into my store."

"Uh-huh."

"If they can't get into my store, I can't sell any books."

"That's the point," one of them shouted. Morse grinned. "That's why we're here."

"You don't want me to earn a living?"

"We don't want you to pander smut."

The protesters cheered. "No smut, no smut, no smut."

Chris hoped it was a police siren he was hearing. "But this is America, Mr. Morse. I'm not doing anything illegal."

"Neither are we." He waved his sign over his head and his group cheered. "First Amendment, baby!"

Chris heard the doors of the police cruiser slam shut. "One last question, please." He gestured to the poster in the window. "Have any of you read *Green Eggs and Ham?*"

"I would not read it here or there."

"I would not read it anywhere!" his supporters chanted." Of course, Chris thought, that part they get.

Morse and his followers backed away as two patrolmen approached. In the other half of his former building, Chris saw several faces pressed to the window, and Queen Kennedy herself trying to clear the space in front of her door.

"Any physical altercation or just noise?" The police sergeant was a solid, barrel-chested man, older than Chris.

"No, but they—"

"—no harm, no foul," the younger officer said. Chris thought he should know him but couldn't remember his name.

"There was harm," he said quickly. "I had to cancel my event. No one could get through their line."

The older cop said, "They have a right to protest."

"But—"

"—and you have a right to run your business."

Chris caught Kennedy's eye and waved her over.

"What we need to do here," the sergeant continued, "is compromise."

"That sounds right." Kennedy extended her hand and introduced herself to the older officer. "Hey, Gino," she said to the other one.

"But you couldn't run your business either, could you?" Chris demanded. "Right?"

The officers kept their eyes on her. "Actually, we couldn't. It was quite the disruption."

"Thank you," Chris said. Kennedy nodded, keeping her smile on the officers.

"Gino, would you ask Mr. Morse to join us?" The younger man trotted down the block where Morse had gathered his people.

"So then, sergeant, it's OK for them to block my storefront? Our storefronts?"

Gino returned with Morse.

"No, it's not OK." To the protester he said, "Sir, we have been over this several times with you. You may protest, but you may not close down his business."

"The people have spoken, officer. We have to do the will of the people." He waved to the crowd and his supporters cheered.

"Mr. Morse, control them or you will join them in jail." Morse waved his arm and the noise abated. "You knew better. You have supporters and he has customers." The sergeant waited for Morse to look at him. "One hour. You get one hour a day to march around with your little signs. Up and down the sidewalk, but not blocking the door. Either door."

"You," he said, indicating Chris, "don't need to contact them at all. Just call us if it gets out of hand, or your customers can't get in."

"But—" Chris looked for support from Kennedy, but she had disappeared. As usual.

The sergeant stared him down. "I know you lost out

today, Mr. Lennox, but you'll think of something."

The crowd dispersed and several people actually entered the bookshop. But not the young mothers and the little ones. He'd have to ask Chloe and her teammates to reschedule.

Brenda met Kennedy as she re-entered the HQ. "See what I mean? You take a stand and you make enemies." She jerked her thumb at the bookshop and her jaw at Kennedy. "He loses business, we lose votes."

Kennedy looked down at her as she passed by. "Democracy is messy, Brenda."

"Messy? This isn't about messy, it's about losing votes."

"It's about a difference of opinion," Kennedy said calmly, and plopped into a free workstation. Volunteers were pounding keyboards on either side of her. She spun the chair around. "Kind of like an election, right?"

"More like sticking your hand into a beehive," Brenda spat. "All you're gonna do is get stung."

"That's not all that's gonna happen," Kennedy replied. "Actual change might occur. You know, like it's supposed to in a democracy."

"This isn't about change, Ms. Phillips, it's about winning an election." Brenda jammed her tiny fists onto her tiny hips.

Kennedy thought to challenge her but smiled instead. Daddy would be proud.

"And the book guy next door?" Brenda's voice pitched higher. Like steam from a kettle. "He didn't like the change. Probably didn't sell one book today. I saw customers leave."

"I don't know." Kennedy kept her voice level. Never let them see you sweat.

"No, and he had to cancel an event."

"They came up with a compromise, Brenda. The protestors are limited to an hour and have to keep the door, both doors open. I think that's fair."

Brenda shook her head. "He lost sales. He took a stand and lost money. What part of that don't you get?"

Chris had stood up for himself, hadn't he. Kennedy tried to recall him from high school and shook her head. "All this is because you don't want Rassy to take a stand, right? Because he'll lose."

The dark-haired nymph raised her arms in mock triumph. "See, I knew you'd get it!"

Kennedy waited for her pirouette to stop. "That may be how it works wherever you're from, but not here. They'll argue and fight about it here in Quaints-ville, but they will vote. If you don't take a stand, you won't get a single vote. Not in Benton Center. Not in Conway County. They will ignore you until you leave."

Brenda dropped her arms and huffed her way through the volunteers to the office. Kennedy smiled when she heard the door slam and spun back to her computer. Gotcha.

Chapter 17

"Yeah, so there I was, surrounded by screaming protesters. Signs waving, insults flying." Chris looked at the Ladies gathered around the table in the Pot & Flagon. "The SWAT team on the scene."

Sammi clapped her hands. "I missed all the fun."

Gena furrowed her brows and squinted.

Across the table Kennedy said, "It was two cops and one squad car."

"Riot gear though, right?" Chris held out his hands. "I'm sure I saw batons and shields and tear gas."

Kennedy took a last drink of latte and let him continue to hang himself. "No."

Chris coughed and gave Sammi a nudge. "Still must have some left in the old lungs." He coughed again.

"Is any of this true, Kennedy? You were with—"

"—it was the two of us, against a mob. Two small business folk, entrepreneurs trying to get ahead, in a sea of anarchy." Gena ignored him.

"Yes, I was there for a while," Kennedy said as she stood up. "Not *with* him, with him."

The older woman looked to Teddi and they both shook their heads. Kennedy was not fooling either of them.

Chris enjoyed the pained look on Kennedy's face. "See? Just like she said, we faced adversity together."

"Not really." She started for the door. "Wait a second, dear," Teddi said, and she stopped.

"We kinda dropped the lede, didn't we? This whole thing was about book banning." Teddi nodded around the table. "We already know Chris' position. Where does your candidate stand on the issue?"

Before Chris could interrupt, she spun toward the door and flung, "Still working on it" over her shoulder.

Teddi and Sammi looked disappointed. Gena said, "That's about what I expected." Mary Jane and several others agreed. Chris tried to speak and was hushed.

"A candidate should have an opinion, ladies." Teddi said. "No matter what it is, we all agree on that, don't we?"

"But—"

"We know where you stand, Chris," Gena said. "You want to sell more books so you're against banning."

Chris tried again, "But—"

"It's your business," Sammi agreed. "Selling books."

"What I don't understand is Kennedy." Mary Jane tapped her wedding ring on the edge of her mug. "I rarely agree with her, but she shot out of here like she had more important things to do than talk to us."

"It's her right," Maggie said.

"True, it is, but it's also her job to put Rassmussen in the best possible light. He has to have a stand on the issue. He can't just go around looking nice."

"He does!" Sammi practically swooned. "I love his eyes."

It's like being in school, Chris thought and raised his hand. "Excuse me?"

Seven faces turned on him. He could feel all fourteen eyes. "I have a thought. Two actually."

Gena sighed. "Put your hand down."

"Yes, well first of all, you don't know my take on book banning. Of course I want to sell more books, but it's about more than that."

The Ladies shook their heads as one. "No, you're a capitalist."

"Your second thought?" Teddi smiled encouragingly.

Chris knew enough to take what he could get and returned their looks with a smile. "I think you're mis-reading Kennedy."

"Barbie with a briefcase." Gena said. "Politico Barbie." Several of them giggled.

"I've been overhearing them arguing about it. I hate it that I can, but the partition is so thin." Chris shook his head. "She's the one trying to get Rassmussen to make a decision. She wants him to take a stand."

They gazed at him blankly. "I know, I know. Airhead. Lights on but nobody's home. I get it."

Chris leaned forward and looked into women's eyes. "She's working hard. In there day and night, and I wouldn't believe it either, but I heard her say it. Several times. She's hot about him not standing up."

"I thought she only had the job because of her father's money," Gena said.

"I can't rule that out." Chris grinned. "But as your spy, you have to at least hear my information, right?"

Gena bored her eyes into his. "This has nothing to do with your feelings for her, does it?"

Sammi gasped. Chris stood up. "And on that note, I take my leave."

"You're saying you have no feelings for her?" Mary Jane called as he opened the door.

"I'm saying we live in parallel universes."

The Gossip Club lowered its collective head and drew closer. This was a tasty morsel indeed.

Chapter 18

Chloe followed Chris through the narrow aisles to his office. As he fell into his green leather chair, she perched herself on the edge of the massive desk.

"Make yourself at home," he mumbled.

"I have news, and besides, I'm family."

"Sorta."

"Third cousin counts as family."

I lose every conversation I have with every female. Chris sat up straighter. "Sorry about having to cancel your kids' book club."

"No problemo, Boss." She blew a pink bubble with her gum. "We'll try Sunday afternoon."

"Other girls OK with that?" He watched her daintily shove the gum back into her mouth.

"Sure, got three, should be enough." She popped another bubble. "Before you even say it, no, of course, there is no gum chewing with the clients."

"But with family?"

"Family understands." Chloe leaned forward in mock seriousness.

"Sorta," he said.

"Yes!" She bounced off the desk and stopped in the doorway. "Hey, at least she helped you with the crazies."

"What? Oh, you mean Ms. Phillips?"

"Yeah." She scrunched up her face. "Ms. Phillips? That's weird."

"How so? It's her name."

"She's a hottie, Boss, and you know it."

"So I shouldn't use her name?"

"How old are you? If you keep this up, you'll lose your status as Funcle."

"I will always be your fun uncle, and anyway, I'm your boss, remember that."

"What ever." She took a step out of the office.

"Wait, Funcuz."

"That's not even a word." Chloe tried to harness her smile. "And yes, funcle is totally a word."

"You said you had some news? Something important?"

She took several hard chews on her gum. "Oh, yeah. Board meeting. You should go."

Chris raised his eyebrows. "Mental telepathy not so much. Talk to me."

"Yeah, so the Board of Education is meeting next week to talk about book banning and all that. You should go."

"Why is that?"

"Books, duh." Chloe shook her head at him. "You sell books, they read books in school and now they want to take books out of school."

"You know that how?"

"Cathy's mom is on the Board of Ed. She says because of how many people are coming, and everybody's all up in arms about it, they're going to have police there and everything."

Chris pursed his lips. "That's not really me. All those people."

"You don't have to talk or anything." When he didn't respond, she said, "Well, I want to go."

"Ask your mom about that."

Chloe's face lit up as she nodded toward the campaign office. "I know, you should bring your tenant. She helped you out with Mr. Morse. I bet she'd go if you asked her."

"Ask her? Like a date?"

Chloe waved her hand in dismissal. "You are *so* old."

A warm laugh bubble escaped him but evaporated like her footsteps down the hall. He had asked Kennedy for a date, several times in fact, in high school. Chris glanced sharply at the door as if someone could be listening in to his thoughts. In fact, she had never turned him down, she'd never said no.

She'd always had an excuse, another date, a visiting aunt, extra cheerleading practice, one time a dog bite, sometimes the flu. She'd love to go out with him if she only had the time. He'd parsed every word she'd ever said to him, and she'd never said no.

She'd never said yes, either, except in his mind. His recollection to the Ladies about Morse and the book banners had been more wish than fact, but the thought of them together, battling together, was still strong. Though he'd told the story with a smile on his face, he'd meant it. He'd always mean it.

Chris pushed the old thoughts from his mind and picked up the stack of mail on his desk. He flipped through the envelopes and stopped when he saw another one from BazillionBooks. He slumped back in his chair and he scanned their latest offer for his store and property.

With that kind of money, he thought, I wouldn't have to worry about books, or book banning, or the Gossip Club. Kennedy either.

Chapter 19

Kennedy tapped a few more keys, left the precinct map on the screen, and spun her chair around to face the semi-circle of volunteers. "That may be a little more detail than you need right now, but you guys are going to be my captains, and I want you to see how the whole process works."

"It's pretty clear, ma'am. Thank you."

Kennedy returned the smile but was still having a hard time realizing she was the intended ma'am. "Is it clear enough for you to be able to explain it to others?"

There were eight volunteers in the group, two men, three women and three college kids. They nodded assent.

"If our recruiting is as good as I think it will be, you'll each have a team and a section of the county." They nodded again. "Oh, and if you can bring a couple of friends, we won't need to recruit so much."

She asked for questions, then brought her hands together. "Remember. Don't get in arguments. Let the literature speak for itself if you're not comfortable." She sharpened her eye contact. "We have a great candidate. Let Senator Rassmussen do the heavy lifting. You're passing out *his* words. OK? Out you go!"

The volunteers picked up their packets of flyers, maps and signs, and filed out. Behind her Kennedy heard clapping. She turned to see Brenda and Scott emerge from the HQ office.

"Into the breach they ride!" Scott laughed at his wit.

"Boldly going where no man has gone before!"

Kennedy attacked her thumbs with her index fingers and put on a fake smile. At least they're going out and doing something, not sitting around and waiting for donations. "You two ready for our meeting?"

"Actually, we were on our way out."

Kennedy leveled her eyes at Scott. "Ten minutes."

He turned to Brenda. "We got time?"

She looked up from her phone. "If we hurry."

Kennedy wasn't sure if the woman sighed or if she'd imagined it. "Great, right over here."

She led them to a round table and picked up her clipboard. "OK, the first thing is, I need signatures to pay for the print ads. It's in your pile Scott, then Brenda can counter-sign."

"All set and organized, I see." Brenda smiled thinly. "But I thought we were still *discussing* print ads."

"Scott?"

"No, these are the base ads. What we need to discuss is color and bigger buys." He signed and handed the document to Brenda. She sighed this time for sure, then signed her name.

"Anything else?" Brenda didn't look up as she spoke.

"Scott, we need to re-schedule the presser. Like we talked about."

"There's no hurry," Brenda said.

"Some of the media outlets in the county are weeklies. Like the papers." Kennedy gestured to the ad buys. "We need more time than in a major market."

"We have time," Scott said and stood up. "I'm on it."

Kennedy kept her eyes on him as she rose. "And your position statements?"

"Don't nag the man, Ms. Phillips."

Before Kennedy could speak, Scott laid his hand on her forearm. "I'm on it." He turned to Brenda. "Let's go. We got places to be and people to see."

Kennedy followed them out to the sidewalk. "It's a lovely spring day. You two going to take a stroll around the Square? Press some flesh and kiss some babies?"

Brenda looked quizzically at Scott. He nodded and said, "We'll get to that, KK. As for now we have some bigger fish to fry."

"I know some folks in these here parts," Brenda drawled. "Got themselves some disposable income."

Kennedy was confused by her tone. "The campaign could use more funding, I'm sure, but it's a great day to—"

"Oh, one thing you could do for me." Scott grinned broadly. "Could you ask your dad to set us up with some tee times? It would be good if I could get these donors—"

"—potential donors."

He returned Brenda's interruption with a smile. "*Potential* donors onto the country club? Might be easier to get them to part with some money."

Kennedy wrote a note on her clipboard. "I can ask. Of course, you'll be seeing him next weekend."

"Oh, and on another topic," Brenda smiled coldly. "Did you see where our opponent has set up his county HQ?"

Scott looked down at his feet. Kennedy waited.

"Out by our hotel, the interchange. In that snappy

new strip mall."

"The strip by the gas station or the one by Taco Bell?" Kennedy returned the campaign manager's lack of warmth. "They're so similar I get them confused."

Scott snorted. "The one without any trees or the one without any shade?"

"Your point?" Brenda didn't smile along with them.

"Why is that a better choice than here?" Kennedy asked. "I'm sure the rent is higher."

"Like I said before. They can get to anyplace in the county faster than we can. It's not so—" Her voice dropped as she gazed around the Square. "I don't know, so out of the way."

"Great," Kennedy said. "They can fly from freeway interchange to interchange. But no one lives out by the interstate highway. They live in small towns miles from the freeway. Like here."

Scott took a step forward. "Brenda, why don't you go bring the car around?" Brenda looked from him to her before marching off.

"You two have to get along."

"She's an idiot."

Scott took a breath. "Look. You each have a different perspective. I can benefit from both." Kennedy looked sharply at him. "The campaign can benefit from different ideas." He clasped his hands together. "Divergent POVs uniting in one great cause."

The black Suburban honked before Kennedy could respond. Scott opened the door and turned to Kennedy. "These meetings may go long, so I might bunk down at one of the rooms we have out at the interchange."

Brenda leaned across the seat. "We got a whole floor of rooms. You ought to come out and see them."

Kennedy looked from her pixie face and velvet coif

to his wavy hair and strong chin. "So you won't be at the BNB?"

"Maybe, maybe not. Have to see how it goes. These guys have some major coinage to spend."

"And you're giving them a chance to spend it."

"It's the American way, darling." He pecked her cheek and jumped into the SUV.

Probably no reason to have your position statements in order then, is there, Senator?

She saw Chris standing on the sidewalk in front of the bookshop and dropped down onto a sunlit park bench. No need to get into it with him, right after this. She closed her eyes and let the spring warmth set in.

Chapter 20

Chris wished his latte would never end and he could sit in the spring sunshine the rest of the day. The rest of his life. He took a small sip to preserve what was left in the cardboard cup.

It was nice here in the Square. Trees budding, kids dragging their parents around, frisbees flying. Laughter. How long had it been since he'd had a good laugh? His eyes flitted around the park and landed automatically on the gold letters in the dark green Lennox Family Bookshop sign. Half a bookshop. Not even half the normal monthly sales.

He finished the latte in a gulp and got to his feet. Depending on a bunch of teenaged softball players to jumpstart his business. I want things to be like they've always been. He sighed. But I can save face by cashing a pretty big check if I sell. The town will understand. I won't be the first businessman to sell out.

He stopped at the crosswalk. But I can't save face

from myself. I'm a sell-out. I'm the last Lennox. As he crossed the street he looked up and down the block. At least Morse and the crazy picketers aren't around. Maybe Chloe's Book Club will be a success. He had to smile recalling his cousin grease-painting those words backwards on the front window. They'd laughed till they cried. See, he reminded himself, that was a good laugh.

He paused at the door to the campaign HQ. Before nine on a Sunday was a strange time to see the lights on and the computer screens glowing. Kennedy was typing and speaking into a cellphone tucked between her neck and shoulder. He had to give her credit; she was there 24/7.

He stepped into his bookshop. "You guys gonna be ready on time?"

Chloe appeared at his side, scissors in one hand and a pack of green construction paper in the other. She and the other three girls were wearing their Benton Center High School softball uniforms; white tops with green pinstripes and stretchy green pants with a wide yellow stripe. "No sweat, boss. We got this."

"Sorta." It looked like a bomb had gone off in a stationery shop.

"We'll read the book over here, do the crafts over there on the tables, and present the grand finale in front of the window."

"Dare I ask?"

"Sure. We're making—well, the kids are making and we're helping—the props, and we're all going to read the book together. Like a play."

"These are little kids, Chloe, they can't read."

"Of course. Watch this. Hey girls." Her three friends joined them, each holding her hands behind her back. "Do you like green eggs and ham?" Instead of saying the nouns, Chloe held up cutouts of them.

The three girls responded, "I do not like, green eggs and ham," holding up the pictures as they said the words. All four then convulsed in laughter.

"It's like they're reading," Cathy explained. "It's called pre-reading." Cathy's mother sat on the Benton Center School Board.

"That's pretty cool." Chris nodded. "They make the props and hold them up at the appropriate time. I like it."

"Eventually they'll see how the letters represent the pictures," Cathy continued. "And it's not like school, it's fun."

"The moms will help, too." Lizzie, the softball team's pitcher added. "They can do it all by themselves at home."

"I suppose a Tik Tok or YouTube video is part of this, right?"

"Absolutely," Cathy said, then to Chloe, "He's not out of it so much."

"This is terrific, girls. I mean it. Thank you." Chris started for his office. "Wait, a question. Sammi, you guys know her, Mrs. Yoder? She said she was coming."

"That's fine," Chloe said doubtfully.

"Yeah, well, she doesn't have a child, but she's pregnant."

"That is so cool!" Cathy bounced on her toes. "The baby can hear inside the womb!"

"Really? I know Sammi loves to perform, but the baby can hear?"

"Duh. Liquid conducts sound waves, right?" Chloe was obviously put out by having to explain common knowledge to her former funcle. "Amniotic fluid? You've heard of it?"

Chris raised his hands in mock surrender. "OK, OK, you guys got this. Let me know if you need anything. I'll be in my office."

A smile returned as he reached his office. All he had to worry about was keeping the sidewalk clear, and it looked like the crazies weren't showing up. Down the hall the girls were chanting, "house, mouse, box, fox, here or there, anywhere, and Sam-I-am." He wondered again how anybody could find smut in that book. It was silly and repetitive, but smutty?

Chloe's Book Club yesterday had gone over even better than anticipated, and Chris was in a great mood as he tinkled the bell and entered the Pot & Flagon. "Morning, Teddi, the usual, if you please."

"Scone and latte coming up," the barista/owner said with a broad smile.

Sammi waved to him, and Chris sat between her and Maggie. They were poring over a video playing on Sammi's phone. He leaned back so all of them could see.

"This is so cute!" Sammi nudged him. "You're on the floor with them. All those little ones reading together!"

Gena glared from across the table. "They're too young to read. They're just repeating."

"They're saying the right words in the right places," Maggie said. "Pretty much like reading."

"Besides they're having so much fun,"

"Not as much as you're having, Samantha." Chris pulled back as Maggie playfully punched her friend. "You're making ears around your baby bump."

"So she can hear. She wants to play with the other kids."

"She's not even born." Mary Jane grimaced and looked to Gena for confirmation. "She can't play with anybody."

The mayor's secretary gritted her teeth. "They think

learning to read is supposed to be fun?"

Teddi quieted them with a stern look.

"Wait, you know it's a girl?"

Sammi beamed. "I can feel it, Chris. I just know."

"It's a mother thing," Maggie said. "It's beyond science."

Gena loudly cleared her throat and the others looked up. "Speaking of hard science, which none of this is." Mary Jane and the pinch-faced woman agreed. "Other than racking up vast quantities of *likes,* whatever those are, what did the event yesterday accomplish, Mr. Lennox?"

Her attempt at taking control of the group was successful, as everyone focused their attention on Chris. "On the affective side, as Sammi has so eloquently elucidated—"

"English, please."

He realized she was Mrs. Morse. "Yeah, it was so much fun, I joined in myself. Good number of people, and if the word spreads, we'll have more next time."

Gena and Mary Jane exchanged looks. Teddi smiled.

"And secondly, on the business side, we sold a lot of books. A bunch of other Dr. Seuss books, and some Shel Silverstein. It was a good day."

"That's the good news." Gena waved her fingers over the table. "All this other stuff is fine and dandy, but you're a businessman, and your business had a good day."

Chris nodded. "Chloe and her buddies are all geared up to do it again. We may do it weekly."

Sammi couldn't suppress a giggle. "And it was fun!"

Overcome by the young mother-to-be's infectious exuberance, the others had to laugh as well. Teddi rose to collect the dishes and said, "Do you think you should attend the Board of Education meeting? As a businessman, I mean?"

"Absolutely he should not." Gena responded before anybody else could. "He's a businessman, not a politician."

"But he sells books, and the meeting is all about books." Maggie shook her auburn hair. "He should go."

"At least to hear what's going on. He's a part of the community." This from the other woman he didn't know.

Mary Jane dismissed her with a wave of her hand. "Sell books. Stay out of controversy. With the picketing you have enough problems."

Teddi said, "Chris?"

Chris glanced around the table. He wanted to tell them to butt out of his business but chose diplomacy instead. "Lennox books has been in this community for three generations. I can't not attend."

"They may blame you for the controversy," Gena said.

"They might. I'm an easy target." He narrowed his eyes. "Yeah, at the very least I need to know which way the wind is blowing. I mean if the Board supports those folks picketing my store, I may as well close down."

"That's my husband. Of course they support him."

"I'm sorry, Mrs. Morse." Chris tried not to blush. "Sure they do."

"It would be easier if you didn't go, Chris." Sammi laid a hand on top of his.

"I have to," he said. "I will attend the meeting and see what's up. Gotta support Joanie and the second-grade teachers in any case."

Chapter 21

Scott made a half-hearted grab for the check, but Kennedy dropped the credit card onto the tray and smiled at the waiter. He bowed and disappeared.

"On me, Alligator Arms." She smirked across the linen covered table in the fine dining section of *Glenda's*.

Rassy raised his right eyebrow. Her heart swooned as it usually did. That half wink and the granite-like chin. "OK, it's on us. On the campaign."

"This is a business meeting after all." He kept his eyes on hers and swirled the cream around in his coffee cup.

"It seems like ages." She left the rest unsaid. It was nearly a week, and he must realize it too. A restaurant with no screens, cellphones in pockets and Brenda nowhere in sight.

"We've been busy, for sure." This time he raised both eyebrows. "Got a lot done."

"We had to move fast, especially with Harvey opening his HQ."

"We did. *You* did." He toasted her with the cup.

"You raised a lot of money in a short time. You and Brenda."

"Can't run a campaign without money." The cup wobbled on the saucer as he set it down. "I left you with a ton of work, and I'm grateful."

The waiter returned, she signed the check, then turned to face Scott. "Are we still a thing? You and me?"

"What? Whoa. Why wouldn't we be?"

She watched him closely. "I can't tell."

"I'm really stressed, KK, you know that."

"I am too." She watched him carefully. "I get calls every day about interviews and the press conference."

"I can't be all over Conway County and here at the same time." He looked down at the cup. "I wish I could."

"No, you're right, I'm the target. They know me and they know where I am." She waited for his eyes to meet hers. "The thing is, I can't give them any answers."

"You're doing fine, you really are."

"Is that your opinion or Brenda's?" She watched his eyes focus in realization.

"This is about you and me and Brenda?" He dropped his hands into his lap and slid away from the table. "How could you think that?"

"I never see you without her." She kept her eyes on his and slid her own chair away.

"That's not fair," he said. "We're working together."

She let him squirm before she stood up. "At the hotel."

He scrambled to grab her coat and held it for her. "Not tonight," he whispered.

She stepped away and turned back to him. "Really?"

"Watch me." He held out his arm.

She took it and they weaved their way through the crowded restaurant, past the bar and onto the porch. They were halfway through the parking lot when his phone rang.

"I gotta take this." He jammed the phone onto his ear and turned his back.

"Sure, you do," she said without hesitation and returned to the bar.

Glenda's had been a machine tool shop back in the day. The two-story red brick building squatted on a slope leading to the river. Upstairs was a lounge and bar in front and the fine dining restaurant in back.

Downstairs was the kitchen and a sports bar. The original brick walls had been retained as had the wooden floors. Pools of light showed well on the glossy floor and rugged brick surfaces. The ceilings had been spray-painted flat black, with the pipes and ventilation equipment left in view. The snaky bar surface was stone, translucent when lighted from below.

Kennedy found an open seat at the dining room end of the bar and ordered a gin and tonic. She set her purse on the next stool and laid her coat on top of it. When the drink arrived, she took a long sip and exhaled.

"Long day, ma'am?" The barman finished drying a tumbler.

Kennedy kept her face on her phone until he walked away. *He's tired? I do all the work, and he's tired?* She took another sip.

On the way to the BNB he took a call? Left me in the parking lot?

Does he think I'm stupid? He's going to visit a donor at eight-thirty?

She looked up at a guy in sunglasses and a Guns N' Roses t-shirt. "Does the seat look empty?"

"No one's sitting in it. Yeah."

"My friend's coming." She turned her shoulder away from the guy and held her phone between them.

"Bitch," the guy mumbled and ambled off.

Good looking, but dumber than a box of rocks. That's what Daddy would say. Box of rocks, box of socks, socks on a fox. She took another sip and smiled recalling the event she'd overheard in the bookshop. Fox wearing crocs.

Actually, that's what Daddy *had* said. That and something about a pretty boy politician. I can handle it, she'd said.

She looked around the bar. Axl had gotten lucky and was flirting up a bottle blonde a few stools away. Scott is cute, but there's something missing. He won't take a stand on anything. All he wants to do is raise money. Smile, show off the dimple, work the room, accept the money. Cash, check, Venmo, Pay Pal. Doesn't matter.

Money is more important than his platform. She set down the glass and nodded to the barman. Doesn't really have a platform. She fished a couple peanuts out of the little ceramic bowl.

Money is more important than me. She took a sip from the new drink. I gotta admit it. He's using me to get to Daddy's money. Just like he told me. Just like everybody said. I'm getting played.

But I'm not giving up. I'm gonna get him elected or carry this county at least. They'll see me on his arm. They'll see me smiling. They'll see me as arm candy. Hell, they can call me Barbie for all I care. No one will know what's going on inside, but they'll vote for Scott Rassmussen, and I'll show them that I can organize a campaign. I figured it out all by myself.

She toasted her glass at her reflection in the mirror behind the bar. It would be a greater accomplishment to elect a flawed candidate like Scott, she told herself. "Here's to you, Pops, And to me!"

Chapter 22

The Board of Education building in Benton Center was originally the entire school system. The three-story brick structure had served as grades one through twelve for many years before taking on its current role as the offices of the Benton Center Local School District. There had been four large classrooms on each floor, and the high school was appropriately lodged on the highest.

The floors themselves had been renovated in order as well. The first two now sported drop ceilings with tiles and light fixtures a full three feet lower than they'd been. Wood paneling sheathed the old plaster walls and indoor/outdoor carpet covered the wide oak planks beneath. In the old high school rooms upstairs, the original black slate blackboards still hung in view under the twelve-foot ceilings.

It had been years since Chris had been in the old structure. He'd had no reason to attend a board meeting, and he certainly hadn't expected the place to be so mobbed. After several minutes the crowd in the corridor started to move and he managed to get through the door into the conference room. Eighty seats filled what had been the fifth and sixth grade classrooms, and every one of them was taken. He slid through the crowd and found a space against the marble windowsill.

The crowd was restive. They weren't here to listen to reports from division heads, and they had no interest in Old Business. They were here, in the grand spirit of Benton Center, to express their opinions, this time on removing *Green Eggs and Ham* from the school library. Chris heard a commotion in the hallway. Mr. Morse and his followers were trying to bring their placards into the room, and the guard wasn't allowing it.

At the podium Diane Maybury rapped her gavel. "Quiet in the room and quiet in the hallway, please. We are in session."

The noise subsided and Morse stepped into the room with his pinch-faced wife. "We are merely expressing our opinions, Madame President," he said.

"Your signs will stay in the hall. We have been using these rules of order for many years."

"But our First Amendment rights, Madam President. We are being—"

Her gavel interrupted him. "You may express your opinion, your verbal opinions, during the audience participation portion of the agenda. No signs. See if you can find a space in the back of the room to stand if you wish."

The room grew hotter and the crowd more agitated as they watched the five-member board slog through its agenda. Purchases, hirings, calendars, notices, lunch menus and staff commendations were not why they had assembled here tonight. They fidgeted in their seats trying to find a comfortable spot on the metal folding chairs. Chris jotted notes on the agenda sheet. He picked out the faces of several people he knew in the rows of seats and exchanged sympathetic glances. He didn't see Rick and assumed he was working at the pub.

The clocks on the wall—there was one in each of the two former classrooms—plugged along. Thunk, thunk, thunk, Chris imagining how they would sound. They reminded him of the big wall clock in his office. The crowd groaned as the architect finally snapped off his Power Point presentation of the new concession stand for the football stadium, and was replaced by a man extolling the virtues of the new replacement buses. Several people scurried out the doors and their seats were quickly refilled.

"Now we come to the audience participation portion of tonight's agenda." Maybury snapped the gavel once.

"Madame President." This from a white-haired board member Chris didn't recognize. He thought he might be a dentist. "Doctor Fine?"

"It's nearly nine o'clock."

The crowd groaned louder and drowned him out. She gaveled twice more. "Let him speak."

"I have been informed, by several sources, that we have a record crowd on hand this evening to discuss an elementary curriculum issue." The crowd agreed loudly, and he paused for them to quiet.

"Ban the Eggs, ban the Ham!"

"Mr. Morse—"

Maybury slammed the gavel onto the desk. "We will have quiet! And we will have respect." An off-duty police officer stepped inside the room at each doorway.

"This issue is controversial," Fine continued. "And the board wants to give it the consideration it deserves."

"Let's vote now!" someone shouted from the third row. Chris didn't recognize him.

Maybury gaveled. Fine said, "We have nothing to

vote on, sir. There is no motion before us."

"I got a motion." The man stood up in the middle of the room and extended the middle fingers of both hands. "Vote on this! All of you vote on this!"

Several cheered, most booed and the officers hustled the man out of the room. When it settled down again, Maybury gestured to her colleague with the gavel. "I believe what Dr. Fine is saying, is that we need to give this issue our full attention. Is that correct?"

"It is. We need a special meeting, for this issue only. All sides need to fully express their views." He looked directly into the crowd. "And we need to listen to all sides."

"But we can't have this kind of chaos." Maybury nodded. "Thursday in two weeks. I think we'll need a larger venue, so check the website for the details. We might have to meet in the high school auditorium."

The crowd muttered and murmured, and Chris felt like they were going to erupt again. Maybury gaveled and spoke clearly. "We have a great tradition in Benton Center. We are a participatory democracy. We value our opinions and—" she paused "—we also value the opinions of others." Several audience members agreed, the others mostly sat silently.

"We'll use the procedure we've used in the past. The public expresses its opinions as is its right, and the Board makes the final decision as its duty." Maybury paused to let her words sink in. "To prevent the kind of nonsense we just witnessed, and to ensure everyone has the chance to participate, please express your positions on the removal of *Green Eggs and Ham* from the school libraries in writing.

"You have a week to get your opinions to us, and we don't have to limit debate, like we would in a live meeting. You can express yourself freely without fear of being shouted down. The Board will read all of them, then meet in two weeks to give our decision.

"On your way out, sign one of the clipboards if you are planning to participate." The crowd began filing out of their seats. "Be sure to indicate in the space after your name, whether you will be supporting the removal of the book in question or opposing the ban."

Maybury rapped the gavel, and they closed the meeting. As the audience left the conference room, the board members stayed in their seats. From the back corner of the room, Kennedy watched Chris work his way to the clipboards and sign the form to express his position. At least he has the guts to stand up, she thought.

Chapter 23

Chris was later than usual to the Pot & Flagon the next morning and the only available seat at the big table was between Kennedy and Mary Jane. He hesitated too long, and everyone watched his face redden as he sat down.

Gena didn't give him a chance to collect his thoughts. "You were there last night, weren't you, at the meeting? Care to give us your impressions?"

All eyes were now thoroughly focused on him. He blurted, "At the board of education meeting?"

He heard Sammi's giggle from across the table, and felt Kennedy shake her head. Gena didn't bother to say "duh"; it was written all over her face.

"Well, I like the idea of letting everyone express their opinion, and I love the idea of saying your piece and not getting booed, but it was pretty anticlimactic. I expected an answer."

"You will have to wait two weeks, like we all do, to find out." Mary Jane nodded. "It's worked that way for years."

"It's fair," Gena said.

"But I kinda wanted to hear all the sides."

"Some people just want to put on a show." Kennedy spoke softly and the others strained to hear. "Like the guy that stood up and shouted. That stuff gets in the way of the reasonable opinions."

"I agree." Chris looked at her. "I didn't see you there."

The door tinkled and Teddi approached the table. "Clear your calendars, Ladies. And Mr. Lennox." She grinned broadly beneath her brightly striped turban and pointed out the bay window. "Three o'clock this afternoon in the Square, a flash mob will be demonstrating for the banning of that Dr. Seuss book about the ham and the eggs."

Sammi giggled again. "Ms. Burns, do you even know what a flash mob is?"

"No idea, Mrs. Patel, but it sounds interesting. I'm gonna be there."

Gena leaned across the table toward Chris. "Sounds like your chance to hear all manner of opinions."

"I hope to hear more than one," he said.

"Chloe, you can work if you need the hours, or we can close up the store."

Chris' third cousin looked at the big regulator clock in the bookshop office. "It's not even three."

He was looking through the window at the crowded Square. "All our possible customers are out there."

She joined him. "Look at that!"

Mr. Morse and his wife led a line of placard-brandishing supporters marching on the sidewalk around the Square. The line stretched a full two sides of the green space. The Square itself was perhaps one third full, with people pouring in from all sides.

"That's most of the town. I'm out of here."

"Be careful, Chlo."

"If you want to continue being my Funcle, come on."

Chris grinned as he locked the door behind them and followed her.

From the window of the campaign HQ next door, Kennedy watched the two leave. Chloe quickly disappeared into the crowd, while Chris stepped carefully across the street and let the marchers pass by.

"Alvin, you're in charge," she said. The young man nodded and kept his face on the computer screen. "Be right back."

It was noisier outside than she'd expected. Horns and drums she couldn't see added treble and bass notes to the murmuration of the crowd. The parade of marchers left the sidewalk as Morse spiraled them toward the Gazebo. She pressed in as closely as she could. There was no sign of Chloe or Chris.

Mr. Morse was at the mic inside the gazebo raising his hands over his head. "You all know why we're here. We're not waiting to write out our feelings about *Green Eggs and Ham*."

"No eggs, no ham!"

Morse grinned as the crowd yelled. "That's what I'm talking about. Ban the ham! The eggs too!"

More cheering. Kennedy felt the crowd press tighter around her as they swarmed toward the gazebo. On the stand next to Mrs. Morse, she recognized the man who had been removed from the board meeting.

"You all know why we're banning this book, right?"

The crowd cheered. Morse held up one finger.

"One, it's sexually explicit."

The crowd cheered.

"Two, it contains offensive language."

The crowd cheered before he could speak.

"Three, it's unsuited to the age group!" Morse exclaimed when they calmed down. "You beat me to it!"

Kennedy knew the book was repetitive and the number of words small; she couldn't recall anything close to sexual. The crowd around her surged forward and she struggled to hold her place and let them pass. Looking up she saw someone climbing the steps of the gazebo.

"Let's ban this book like we banned all the other Dr. Seuss books!"

"Ban the ham. Ban the eggs!"

Kennedy noticed Chris approaching the microphone as Morse did. "Unlike the board meeting last night, we are going to let a speaker express his opinion right here, right now, in front of us all.

"In the spirit of democracy, we will hear what I presume is an opposing viewpoint." The crowd strained to hear. "I give you Mr. Lennox, the owner of the Bookshop across the street."

Chris stepped to the microphone. The crowd booed half-heartedly. "Let him speak." Morse had to say it several times before the crowd quieted down. "We're all about free speech."

Chris looked from Morse to the crowd and held up a copy of *Green Eggs and Ham*. "This book by Dr. Seuss has never been banned anywhere in America."

The crowd booed, shouted their dissent, and waved their signs.

Morse grabbed the mic stand. "All his books have been banned somewhere in the country."

"Not true." Chris fought to get back in front of the mic.

"Ban the ham! Ban the eggs!"

"It's smut! It's racist!"

"Have you read it?" Chris shouted back.

"You're just trying to sell books!"

Chris wrestled control of the mic stand. "The author's family pulled six books out of publication—"

"No smut, no sales!"

Kennedy struggled to see what was happening as his voice cut out. Chris disappeared into the mass of people, and the man who shouted at the board meeting was nowhere to be seen.

"That's enough of that nonsense," Morse was saying, and the crowd clapped. "He actually thinks we'd read something like that." The crowd laughed. "Who does he think we are? And saying that this book has never been banned?" Morse shook his head sadly.

"Well, it takes all kinds, and now it's time for me to introduce one of us, our favorite candidate in the primary for the US Senate, Mr. Mike Harvey!"

The crowd clapped for several seconds before respectfully falling silent. Scott Rassmussen's opponent stepped to the mic. Of course, Kennedy thought. *My candidate's off somewhere with Brenda looking for more donations. He should have said the things Chris did.*

"Thank you, Mr. Morse," Harvey said. "I am here to support your position." The crowd roared. "We must protect our children. It is our sacred duty as parents!"

The crowd was quiet, but Kennedy sensed a throbbing tension in them like a pot of water just before boiling. She slipped back away from them and worked around toward the front of the stage. She hoped Chris wasn't in danger.

Chapter 24

Kennedy circled the entire Square before finding Chris slumped on a bench near the WWII howitzer. She stopped in front of him, and he didn't look up. "I misjudged you."

"It's a long way down from Mt. Olympus, KK." Chris spoke without thinking and didn't look at her.

She pouted automatically. "What does that mean?"

"You judge everybody. It's what you do."

"No, I don't." She put one foot in front of the other and her hand on her hip.

He waved his hand as if erasing her comment. "Yes, you do. You gaze down from your lofty throne above and judge the antics of the little people down below."

"That's not a nice thing to say." She refreshed her pout. "I just came looking for you to see—"

His eyes flashed to hers. "You came to gloat. To make sure I made a big enough fool of myself."

"No, I really—"

"You judged that much correctly, at least. They

practically ran me out of the gazebo."

Kennedy uncocked her hip and replaced the pout with a wide smile. Chris wasn't looking. "I thought maybe you were hurt."

"Why would you care?" His voice was faint and his gaze unfocused.

"Why wouldn't I care?"

He turned to her. "I'm invisible to you. I always have been. Why would you care now?"

She caught his gaze and held it. "Because you took a stand."

He didn't respond.

"That's how I misjudged you." She sat down on the bench beside him.

He slid down the park bench. She couldn't tell if he was giving her space or if he wanted to avoid her. "Anyway, not a lot of people have the guts to do that."

Chris screwed up his face. "That's the official verdict?"

"I don't see it as a verdict." She smiled contentedly. "I'm impressed."

"Thank you." His voice low, his eyes away from hers.

"My pleasure."

"Yeah." Rick would advise him to hold back his anger, but he sat up and faced her. "It means so much that the queen herself has deigned to mingle with us lowlifes, let alone praise us."

"Are you mocking me, Chris?"

"No, Kennedy, I'm confused. You say one nice thing and expect we should bow down? It's not like you actually care about Benton Center."

"Of course I do." She reached to pat his hand and he jerked it away.

"No, you don't." She reformed her phony pout, and he couldn't stop himself. "You never cared before, and you don't care now."

"How can you say that? I've made Ben Cen the focal point of a statewide political campaign."

"Yeah, and if your boy Scotty wins, you're out of here as fast as you can. This town is just a steppingstone for you."

"I don't get it. I do the right thing. I admire your bravery in taking a stand, and you still hate me."

"See? That's what I mean. You're doing 'the right thing.' Like you read in a book how you should treat the common folk. Praise them. Pat their little heads. Tell them how swell they are."

Kennedy leapt to her feet. "That's not fair!"

"That's how you've always treated us, me," he snapped in return. "When you even bothered to notice."

"I didn't have to come back here, but I did." She jabbed a finger in his face. "It's my home too."

Chris remained seated on the bench and watched the crowd behind her drifting out of the Square. He looked into her angry blue eyes. "Living here doesn't make you part of the community, KK. Go back to your palace in the sky. Those of us earthbound don't need your help."

Chapter 25

Kennedy hadn't slept well and the run through RiverPark hadn't had its usual restorative effect. She'd pushed herself especially on the inclines, but now as she cooled down in the Square, she just wanted to go back and curl up in bed. Her own bed at home, not the rented BNB. She didn't want to have to explain herself to the Gossip Club, and she certainly didn't want to explain herself to her father.

But the metal Pot & Flagon sign squeaked in the gusty wind and drew her eye as she tried to scurry past. She stopped in front of the bay window and took a deep breath. No, I've got nothing to hide, nothing to be ashamed of. She pulled the door open and entered.

The Ladies were in full voice, and she was able to squeeze into a seat between Sammi and Mrs. Morse under the cover of their enthusiastic, and loud, discussion. Sammi returned her nudge as the woman on the other side said, "Well yes, that's exactly how my husband felt as they kicked him out of the board meeting. That's why he was in the gazebo in the first place."

Kennedy had seen that but wondered about the rough looking man who'd followed Chris from the Gazebo. She wondered if Sammi knew who that man was.

"That's great," Mary Jane was saying. "That's the whole point of a democracy. Getting the different points of view out into the open."

"But they practically carried him out of the board building."

"No, that's not what I saw." Mary Jane looked from Mrs. Morse to Gena. "The police just led him away. It wasn't violent at all."

"It shouldn't *be* violent!"

Kennedy could feel violence pulsing off the woman on her left. She slid her chair a little closer to Sammi.

Teddi spoke in a calm voice. "We have other customers here, don't we. Let's all take a nice, deep breath." She touched each of them with her warm brown eyes. "That's better now, isn't it?"

Several seconds passed quietly. Gena matched her voice to the barista's. "That is better, Teddi, thank you." After several more seconds, she said, "The first point is clarity of positions. After the demonstration yesterday, it is clear that one side favors banning the book. Your husband." Gena nodded to the woman next to Kennedy. "Mr. Morse and Mr. Harvey the candidate for Senate—"

"—and most of the people on the Square."

"Yes, Geraldine. We were there, too, and we read your article in the *Bugle*. That position is clear. But before we can decide, we need to hear from the other side." Gena turned to Kennedy, and the other eyes at the table followed hers.

"Chris, um, Mr. Lennox spoke against banning the book. At the Gazebo. Yesterday." Kennedy felt her face redden but kept her voice mostly under control.

"Yes, he did, and?" Gena's eyebrows raised along with the timbre of her words.

When Kennedy didn't respond quickly, Gena continued, "It would be a help if your candidate, Mr. Rassmussen, would state his position." She gathered nods from the others around the table. "So Benton Center can make an informed decision."

"We're still working out the fine points of Scott's position."

"That's what you said two weeks ago," Mary Jane said. "Well?"

Kennedy straightened up and slid back from the table. "We are holding a press conference during the donor event at the country club."

"Is your Daddy going to write him a big check?" Gena barely kept the sneer out of her voice. Geraldine listened closely. "That's what I hear."

"Scott will answer all your questions then, and everyone will be on the same page." She stood up. "Actually, I'm meeting with him in a few minutes. I'll be sure to mention your concerns."

Kennedy took her plate and cup to the bussing station, and the Gossip Club Ladies drew their heads together like fingers in a fist. As she was tossing her cup into the bin, Teddi appeared at her side. "Follow me."

It was darker in the wine bar, and they could barely hear the ladies in the front of the coffee shop. Teddi motioned to a table by the brick wall, and the two sat down.

"What's wrong?" Teddi asked.

Kennedy pursed her lips. "Wrong? Nothing."

"Girl, don't you lie to me." Teddi glared at her.

Kennedy dropped her glance and her voice. "What

do you mean?"

Teddi patted her hand. "You're not you."

Kennedy looked at her.

"You're not a queen and you're not representing the matriarchy. You're not flaunting the pink and you're not taking charge."

Kennedy nodded. "Somewhere in the middle."

"Neither fish nor fowl." When the younger woman didn't respond, Teddi continued, "You gotta pick one. Start with Mr. Scotty."

Kennedy felt her eyes drifting and sought Teddi's. "I can't get him to take a stand."

"Why not?"

Kennedy straightened up a bit. "He's afraid of alienating the other side. Or offending anybody."

"That's politics." Teddi's eyes flashed in the dim room.

"I know, but that's not the advice he's getting from other places."

"Mmm." Teddi peered over the rim of the coffee mug. "Our Miss Brenda. I thought so."

"Yeah, there's that, and he is overly focused on money. He'd rather fundraise than discuss issues."

"That's no bueno."

"No, especially in Benton Center. Money's not the most important thing around here."

Teddi returned Kennedy's tentative smile. "But there is more going on here than the politics, am I right?"

She had no idea how the older woman knew. "May I ask you a question?"

Teddi settled back in her chair, a turbaned, all-knowing Yoda. "I thought you never would."

"I don't usually ask questions." She smiled thinly as her words poured out. "I don't know how to start. Taking a stand is good, and Chris took a stand yesterday, and he caught a lot of push-back, and I complimented him for it, and I sought him out afterwards in the Square, and I told him he did the right thing."

Teddi held up a palm and said softly. "Take a breath, child."

Kennedy realized the torrent of feelings was pouring from her own mouth and stopped, shocked.

Teddi took her hand in her own. "It's good that you felt comfortable opening up to me." She held the young woman's eyes in a warm gaze.

"But he still hates me!" Kennedy blurted.

"Of course he does."

"But why?" Kennedy was confused. "I told him how I felt, and he hates me!"

Teddi paused to see if she was finished, then said, "Chris stayed, you left."

Kennedy raised her hands, then dropped them into her lap. "I returned. Here I am!"

Teddi smiled. "He thinks you'll leave again."

"That's not certain. I don't know." Kennedy's voice fell off and she looked away. "I might."

"Chris Lennox has bet his whole life, his career, on Benton Center and his family's bookstore. The way things are going, he may lose both."

"I want to help him." Kennedy's eyes snapped back to Teddi's. "But he told me to butt out."

Teddi's eyebrows raised toward her turban. "And?"

Kennedy raised her eyes and spoke softly. "I believe in his stand."

"Good, I'd hoped so." Teddi toasted with her mug. "Problem is, he doesn't trust you."

Kennedy slumped. "High school."

"Yup. Now you know how it feels." The barista set her mug down with a thump and the girl startled. "You know what to do."

"No, I don't." Kennedy let her voice carry her worry. "I really don't."

"High school is over. For both of you." Teddi patted the girl's hand. "You broke out of your shell, KK. Now it's time to jump out of the nest and fly. On your own."

Chapter 26

It was colder than it appeared, the morning mist not yet burned off, and Kennedy wished she wore something warmer than her thin running clothes. She pulled her arms across her chest and continued to stare at the storefront across the street. The double storefront. A delivery van parked and obscured her view. Teddi's words had stung her. Not the words themselves, they were delivered kindly, but the memories they'd disturbed.

Kennedy remembered Teddi scrubbing the floors and bussing the tables of the Coffee Pot. She and her school friends had mostly ignored her; now she was considering the woman's advice. Chris said he'd been invisible to her. Had she treated the barista with respect, or had she been invisible too? She held herself tighter as the wind gusted across the Square.

Teddi knew what she was talking about. Both about local politics and about her. Kennedy let out a breath. The Amazon van left the curb and revealed the Lennox Family

Bookshop. The left side she was renting and the right side where Chris had crammed all the books. Her Dad always told her to face a problem directly. Teddi was telling her to trust herself and fly on her own wings. Could they both be telling her the same thing?

Whatever their advice, she had a problem right now. As Teddi noticed, the Rassmussen campaign was going down in flames and taking her with it if she couldn't get Scott to clearly state his platform. At least solving a problem was better than thinking about how she'd treated Teddi in the past, and much better than how she'd treated Chris. She got up off the park bench.

As Kennedy reached for the door to the campaign HQ, she realized she was still in her running clothes. Scott would notice but not mind, while Brenda would notice and hate her for it. She shunned the thought and opened the door. Alvin, McKenzie the pollster, and a couple volunteers were huddled in front of their computer screens. Brenda and Scott looked up from the conference table. He smiled, she glared, Kennedy said, "Sorry I'm late. Got caught up in local politics."

"Looked to me like you were nodding off on a park bench." Brenda looked to Scott for agreement.

"Huh?" Scott didn't return her look.

Kennedy pulled her tablet and a yellow pad from the desk and spoke without making eye contact. "Meeting with my local focus group, Brenda. Then weighing their input."

"The gossip girls, right? Is that what you call them?" Brenda smirked.

Scott looked up from his cell. "Is this going to take long? We have a meeting in a half."

Kennedy refused the bait from both of them. "The Ladies, as I call them, have their fingers on the pulse of the community. They know what's going on, so they're a good source of information."

"McKenzie," Brenda called, and the long-haired mathematician promptly placed a laptop in front of her. She rotated the screen to show Kennedy and the candidate. "We have the demographics right here. The figures show what's going on in the area. Thank you, Mac." She turned the computer back around and arched her eyes to Rassmussen.

Scott said, "It can't hurt to hear the input, can it, Brenny? I mean, we can always use some more intel."

Brenda sighed and settled her hands in her lap. "Well?"

Kennedy looked at Scott's blue eyes and chiseled features. He brushed a sheaf of dark blond hair from his forehead. He was gorgeous, and he had called her 'Brenny.' She said calmly, "You have to be part of the community, Scott."

"But I'm not."

"That's why we hired you," Brenda said with a sloppy grin at McKenzie. "You're the native."

Kennedy kept her eyes on the candidate. "I'm saying you have to act like you're a part of the community. Be accessible to them."

"I have to be who I am, Kennedy. That's what you always tell me."

She could feel the gloat emanating off Brenda like heat from a feverish child. She pursed her lips. "What I mean is, you have to share their values or at least be conversant with them."

Brenda closed her laptop with a snap. "I thought you were all about position statements and issues and white papers."

Kennedy kept her eyes focused on Scott, not the annoying woman. "I am, that's how you share their values.

The people of Benton Center and Conway County value democracy above all. They won't make a decision unless they can hear both sides."

"This again." Brenda sighed theatrically and nodded at Rassmussen, then McKenzie.

"Why should I take a stand on book banning, Kennedy? Mike Harvey staked out the pro side, so automatically I'm the con, right?"

"If that is the position you want to take. Are you against banning *Green Eggs and Ham* from the second-grade classroom?"

"That's not what I said."

"If he does that, all those folks in the Square will vote *against* him." McKenzie tapped his screen as if applauding Brenda. "Hear, hear."

Kennedy responded with an edge but controlled her pitch unlike the campaign director. "And all those folks who are against banning the Dr. Seuss book will vote *for* him."

Scott held up his hands. "Ladies, please. I have a question." He looked from one to the other until they nodded. "OK then. My question is, who gets hammered?"

"The nail that sticks out." Brenda grinned like a kid answering her teacher's question. "Every time you stick your head out, you get hammered."

Kennedy gritted her teeth at the practiced response. "Well, then, I see that you three are in agreement." She jotted something on the yellow pad before dropping it in her bag. "As you know, I've arranged for a press conference Saturday night at the BiggInsCo donor event. I'm sure they will ask for clarification on your book position and others as well." She smiled at Scott. "It will be a perfect time for you to make a clear statement."

He didn't respond. Brenda extended her arms to

include the candidate and the pollster. "We'll think about it."

Chapter 27

The shower felt good to Kennedy. Not only was she sluicing the warm, soapy water across her body, she was shrugging off some of the doubt that plagued her worse than dried sweat. She turned off the water, slid the shower curtains aside and stepped carefully over the steep side of the old-fashioned tub. As her toes dug into the deep pile of the bathmat, she reached for the thick towel and told herself again she was doing the right thing.

The wrong thing—well, one wrong thing, of course— would be to show up at her father's office in her workout clothes. She agreed with that piece of her father's advice, knowing from experience what effect the proper outfit had on others. She could see the symbolic nature of a costume change today as well, but that was where her doubts lay.

It's not as if I have to decide this very minute, she thought as she wrapped a hand towel around her thick blond mane. I can just kinda sorta pick his brain. Get him talking about his two favorite subjects: his daughter and how to run a business.

As if her father wouldn't see through her plans. Like she could trick him. She rubbed a hole on the foggy surface of the little mirror over the sink and stuck her tongue out at the goofy woman staring back at her. Right, kinda and sorta. Speak to him like he's not the only adult in the room, the woman told her. For once.

She had managed to move most of her clothes—well, some of her clothes—to her room in the BNB and stood now in front of the antique wardrobe. It had warmed up since her early morning run, and it was nearly the end of April, and darn it, it was spring: she pulled a colorful print dress off the hanger.

Minutes later in her car, the real doubts returned. They didn't barge in and attack like they often did at night. They lurked at the edge of her mind and snatched little bites from her confidence. Just enough to let her know they were there. She turned the radio up and adjusted the window a bit. She wouldn't let the doubts spoil her day, and the spring breeze would give her hair the look she wanted. It paid to get a good haircut.

She wanted to project the right image and had set up the meeting with her father in his office, rather than at lunch or home. She had called his secretary to get on the calendar instead of dropping by as she usually did. Those were what he would expect from a business colleague, and she was sure of those choices.

But the real doubts continued to nibble away at her confidence as she parked in the space next to the Grantham Phillips CEO sign, and she used the snap of her heels on the terrazzo of the lobby to chase them back to their dark corners. When the elevator chimed and the door opened, she strode across the lush carpet, announced herself to his secretary, and waited to be called into his office. Not like a daughter, but a business colleague.

Kennedy heard the intercom on the secretary's desk buzz but waited to be led to the office door. As they waited for her knock to be answered, Sherri said, "Nice dress. Springy." They shared a smile and the door opened.

"Ms. Phillips, is it?" Her father raised his eyebrows but didn't smile. "Have we met?"

"Daddy!" she exclaimed, but carefully walked to one of the upholstered chairs in front of his enormous wooden desk. "Many times, as you well know."

"I thought maybe, on the settee? Where we usually—"

"This is business, Daddy." She seated herself and pulled a file from her bag.

"Business. Daddy," Grantham muttered under his breath as he sat in the chair opposite.

She raised her eyebrows at him.

"What, I have to sit behind my desk? I do conduct business here, too."

She gave him a several seconds before saying, "No, this is fine."

"Glasses," he said. "Dark rimmed, maybe oval."

She chased the nipping doubts into the darkness, slowly turned to her father and gave him her best steely glare. "Because I am too good-looking to be taken seriously?"

"No, I—"

"Because if that's what you're saying, I might as well leave." She accented each word equally and kept her eyes on him as she placed her bag on the floor beneath her chair.

"OK, OK, I know you want to talk business, but you're my daughter and you look like you've got it all together. And . . ." His voice faded, and he smiled weakly. "Let's start over, shall we?"

After she nodded, he said, "So then, Ms. Phillips, what brings you here today?"

She snapped the file folder onto her knee. She'd seen him do it before and knew he'd like it. "Scott Rassmussen, senatorial candidate, the May primary in a couple weeks."

"Running against Mike Harvey."

"That's correct." Kennedy opened the folder and wondered for an instant if glasses might actually be a good prop. "As I am his campaign coordinator for Conway County, we have previously discussed the amount of a donation BiggInsCo would be prepared to make on his behalf."

Grantham bunched his bushy white eyebrows together. "We are merely discussing the amount?"

"Yes sir. You committed to a donation on—" She scanned her notes although she knew the date. "—on the 23rd of March. At a meeting in the Club, I recall."

Kennedy watched him nod and not smile. "You're asking me to write him a big check. I assume that's what campaign coordinators do."

She waited to be sure he was not baiting her again. "As a matter of fact, no."

Her father's eyes bore into hers, as she'd hoped. "Your campaign doesn't need the money? I find that extremely hard to believe."

The doubts ran away as she heard him use "extremely" instead of "very". He only did that when he was, well . . . extremely interested.

"What I'm here for today is two checks, not one."

"Wait, you want more money? I assumed you were flush."

She smiled to herself, not to him. "I want a large check and a small check."

A puzzled look traced a path across Grantham's face, followed by a satisfied one. He began to smile, then stopped.

"A you're-my-guy size and a thanks-for-participating

size."

"You have doubts about him, don't you."

She held his eyes. "I do."

He thought for a moment. "Do you want to talk about it?"

"If you're asking if I want your advice, Mr. Phillips." She paused. "At the present time I don't. You have given me an opportunity and prepared me for it."

Kennedy had seen him try and keep his enthusiasm in check before and fail miserably at it. She adjusted the papers in her folder until he composed his face. "I don't suppose you want to tell me what hurdle you want Rassmussen to jump over."

"No, sir, I do not."

His eyebrows bunched again. "This is dangerous, Kennedy." He held up his hand as she began to speak. "Let me just say this. You must know you will lose your job if you give him the small check."

She nodded.

"You may lose a lot more than just *this* job. The word will get out." He held her gaze. "Maybe I'm giving money to the wrong candidate."

"Maybe he'll come around." She kept his gaze. "But either way I have to do the right thing, Daddy. Sir."

Grantham pulled his checkbook from his suitcoat. He didn't react to her choices of address but nodded thoughtfully as she said, "It's the way you taught me."

Chapter 28

Chris stared through the window of his cramped little bookshop at the park bench where Kennedy had accosted him. He'd handled it badly and let his anger control his reaction. Now he ignored the budding greenery and the kids playing and the people walking their dogs and focused on the bench. It sat alone, like he was. In the middle of springtime activity, but not part of it. Seeing Chloe coming across the street, he retreated into his office.

She found him anyway. "Hey Funcle! It's great out there, you should come out." She crinkled her nose at the dim, faintly musty office before plopping down on the chair. "It's gross in here."

"Nice to see you, cuz." He forced a wry smile. "Why are you so happy?"

"It's spring." Chloe looked at him as if he were the dumbest man on the planet or a recent visitor to it. "Duh."

She drew the word out into four syllables, and Chris had to laugh. He raised his hands. "OK, I give up.

Talk to me."

She narrowed her focus to his face. "OK. As practically your only living family member, it's my duty anyway, but since you asked."

Chris waved his fingers as if brushing the dust off his desk. "I can't wait to hear."

Chloe settled back in the chair, furrowed her brow and sighed. "Uncle Chris, you are a recluse."

He thought quickly. "A brown recluse arachnid?"

"I'm serious." She shook her head and didn't smile. "I'm worried about you."

He stopped humming the Spiderman theme as he recognized his mother's face across the desk. "I'm fine, Chlo."

"I know you've been stressed about the move and saving the bookshop." The girl's hands dropped to her lap. "But you can't just sit here in the dark."

"Get out and enjoy the nice spring weather? I did that yesterday, and they booed me off the gazebo. They got crazy in a nanosecond."

"You did the right thing, Uncle C." She peered into his face and smiled. "I'm proud of you."

He grinned weakly. "Thanks, cuz."

"However." Chloe's voice was too big for the tiny office. "There is another issue we need to discuss."

"You sound like my mother. Your aunt." Chris recoiled at her piercing stare and the menacing words. "You realize you're not my mother, don't you?"

"My aunt, yeah, but I can still give you advice." She reached a fist across the desk, and he bumped it with his. "When you need it."

"I am in need of advice?"

"Big time." She giggled, and he relaxed. "What happened in the Square, after the rally?"

"What do you mean?"

"Deflecting. This is gonna be good." She rubbed her hands together. "You and the park bench and your tenant." She jerked her thumb at the HQ next door.

"Nothing. Mom."

The teenager shook her head. "Nice try. I saw you talking, she ran off and you like melted onto the bench. I was so freaked out, I didn't even come over."

"This is what you want to talk about?"

"I understand the stress of the bookstore, but—" She pulled her long legs onto the chair under herself. "What did you say to chase her away?"

"What? Nothing." He looked at the clock, his hands, and finally her face. "I didn't have to. She ran away like she always does. Did."

Chloe's eyes lit up. "Wait. You told me you were in school together, didn't you?"

"Same graduating class, different social classes."

Chloe furrowed her brow. "Cliques. Got it."

Chris was on safer ground when she nodded. "I was invisible to her then, and I still am."

"What actually happened at the rally thingy?"

Chris searched for the words. "She came over and acted all concerned about me. Like she cared or something." His eyes lost their focus, and he shook his head side to side.

"Maybe she did." When she saw his shocked response, she smiled broadly. "Care about you, I mean. I'm a kind of half-full type of gal."

Chris had to laugh. "That you are. Yeah, so she stopped by with a load of crapolla, I was distressed anyway, and I didn't buy it. Case closed."

Chloe considered for a moment. "Maybe not. Maybe she's changed."

"Now she cares about me? This is the girl who hired

a professional voice coach so she could play Lisa in *My Fair Lady*!"

"But—"

"She's the girl who flew to Barbados over Christmas so she could win Best Tan!"

"Well, yeah—"

"Look, she won Homecoming Queen under very suspicious circumstances. But really, Chloe, she only cares about herself."

"Wait." The teenager's eyes arched open. "You liked her!"

"Not the point. Everyone loved her." Chris waved his hand and spoke rapidly to change the subject. "What got me yesterday was she came over and acted like she'd changed."

Chloe's eyes narrowed. "Maybe she has. It's not high school anymore."

He let out a breath and let the bullet pass by. "There's a saying about leopards and stripes or tigers and spots and I get it all mixed up." He smiled at her.

"Nice try, but no."

"What?"

"She is working here on her own. She expressed concern about you. And she is still smoking hot."

"And you think?" He shook his head. "That ship sailed."

"So there *was* a ship."

He glared across the table. "Stop it."

"OK, OK, well, you're not exactly yourself lately, and you don't seem to be scoring on the old social front."

He leaned back in the chair and avoided another bullet. She smiled sweetly. "Just saying. She caught you when you were down and maybe you overreacted."

"Makes sense, but Chloe, you don't understand."

He thought for a bit. "She's not genuine."

"Go on." His cousin was clearly enjoying dissecting his personal life.

"Maybe I am being too critical." He sought out her eyes in the half-darkened room. "I'll put it this way. Kennedy goes out of her way to please people. Everybody. She finds out what makes them tick, then feigns interest and everybody falls for it."

"Maybe she's getting advice from other people." She waved her hands as the idea occurred to her. "Maybe she's not a recluse and doesn't do everything by herself."

He dismissed the idea with a wave of his own. "No, that's not it. She's using them."

Chloe considered. "Maybe she's afraid of failing."

"You may be right; she is a perfectionist. Like her dad. But she's so busy stroking everyone and worrying about pleasing them, you have no idea who she really is." His face gripped as he concentrated. "That's the worst part. I've known her for years, and I don't know her at all."

Chloe nodded sagely. "If you don't know a person, it's hard to trust them."

Chris smiled. "You are a genius."

"You better hope I am." He looked puzzled as Chloe got up out of the chair. "Because you're asking a sixteen-year-old for relationship advice."

The girl disappeared into the narrow hallway before he could disagree.

Chapter 29

The promise of a warm spring was in the evening air, and the white lights in the trees surrounding the patio sparkled. The clicking of cutlery was fading as the hundred or so patrons finished their desserts, took a final sip of white wine, and settled back for the hopefully short campaign speeches. The donor event at the Country Club had gone better than Kennedy could have anticipated, but as she carefully dabbed her lips with a thick white napkin, a doubt scurried into her consciousness and took a bite.

The cocktail hour before dinner had gone smoothly, and as far as she could gather, her candidate had avoided alienating any potential supporters. The upcoming election was a party primary, and candidates from up and down the ticket were working the crowd as well, but only Rasmussen and Harvey would be given the stage to speak. She was afraid of what her candidate would say.

Grantham reached his hand over hers and she looked up. "You've done all you could, Kennedy. The decision is in his hands, not yours."

She smiled her thanks, and the doubt retreated. "He won't see it that way."

"He's a politician. That's par for the course." Her father smiled broadly and winked. "As you well know the 18th green is just beyond those trees."

She pulled her hand free and slapped his. "That's awful." But his dad joke banished her doubt.

Mike Harvey had spoken first, and Scott was just wrapping up his prepared remarks. His bland prepared remarks. The Q and A would be next. Without intending to she thought of Chris.

"Now as I understand it," Scott was saying from the small stage at the edge of the patio. "I believe we have time for a few questions." He nodded to a reporter from the *Benton Center Bugle*.

"Thank you, Mr. Rassmussen, I—"

"That's Senator Rassmussen."

"Yes, um, State Senator Rassmussen—"

"That's right, I'm running for the US Senate." Scott looked deliberately into the crowd. "I know that can be confusing. I wanted to clarify my position on that. Ohio Senate now, running for US Senate." He nodded as if decoding a quadratic equation. "Now then, your question."

"Yes, thank you State Senator." The reporter looked up from his notes. "I wonder if you could clarify your position on the currently controversial issue in Benton Center regarding the banning of schoolbooks?"

"Thank you. I am so glad that you gave me the opportunity to speak about this deeply important issue." His brows contracted in concentration. "I am sure that the good and knowledgeable citizens of Benton Center, the county seat of Conway County as you well know, will make the decision that is best for them." He smiled.

"I am sure they will, Senator, State Senator. But my question is not about the voters, rather about you as the candidate. Are you in favor of banning the book in question or are you not? What is your position?"

Scott held his arms wide. "My position? I'm standing!" He beckoned a laugh with his outstretched hands and got a smattering of applause.

The other reporters at the side of the stage all spoke at once, loudly enough to drown out the weak laughter.

"OK, OK, here it is. My position on this issue and the reason I'm *standing* for election." He loosened his tie and scanned the crowd intently. Kennedy felt like he was looking for her. To blame her.

"I am a uniter," Scott said in his most sincere voice. "I do not wish to be divisive." He shook his head to banish that thought. Kennedy felt her throat tighten.

"There is just too much conflict in our country today. Even in this peaceful county." He nodded as if agreeing with himself. "Too much discord, dissent, and disagreement. That's not me.

"I'm for small government. Let the people decide the issue, not the politicians."

"But your opponent Mr. Harvey—"

Scott smiled down at the *Bugle* reporter. "You're not going to bait me, sir." To the crowd he raised his arm and they quieted. "Thanks for listening. I'm off now to continue my tour of the state to spread the good word. As a famous man once asked, 'Can't we all just get along?'

"To that I say, yes, yes we all *can* get along."

Kennedy dropped an envelope in front of her father and bolted toward the stage. Brenda and McKenzie had left their posts, and she could see them leading, even pulling, Scott away from the crowd. She raced through the lounge to intercept them in the parking lot.

She waved the other envelope over her head. "Don't forget your campaign donation. From BiggInsCo."

Scott let go of the car door and held out his upturned hand.

"My father's a hard man, but he kept his word." She gave him the check.

"Old fashioned," Brenda muttered.

Scott opened the envelope, said something under his breath, and tossed it into the vehicle. "I counted on you, Kennedy. I am surprised and disappointed."

"He wanted to know where his money was going. That's why I told you to take a stand."

Brenda looked from Rassmussen to McKenzie. "We discussed that."

"Tell your daddy thanks." Scott stepped onto the running board of the SUV. Over his shoulder he said, "For nothing."

Kennedy yanked the door out of his hand. "How dare you! This was my decision, not his!"

"What? You work for *me*, and you lowballed me?" Scott smiled smarmily. "No way. No, you're covering for your old man." Beside him, Brenda glared, and McKenzie's eyes darted randomly.

"No, Scott, this was my call. I gave you good advice and you listened to these two." She looked neither at the manager nor the pollster.

Scott grabbed Brenda's hand, either in friendship or to keep her from hitting Kennedy. "You know, at the end of the day, it really doesn't matter."

"It does matter." She returned his cold stare.

Brenda slid across the middle seat of the black van and Scott climbed in behind her.

"Don't worry," Kennedy said to his back. "I'll fulfill my contract with the campaign and keep the HQ open.

The canvassing will continue."

The State Senator pulled the door closed between them. The window slid open. "You had better deliver every single fricking vote in Conway County, Miss Phillips, or you will never work in this business again." The window rose, and the SUV roared away.

Chapter 30

Chris hadn't slept much. As he tossed and turned, his mind replayed scenes from Chloe's brash assurances of Kennedy's interest, to the woman's obliviousness of him at all. From pillar to post, his mother and Chloe's aunt had always said. When morning finally arrived he had dragged himself into the office in the desperate thought that going over bills would be better.

It had been worse. His revenues showed several peaks, actual days with good volume, but overall sales were down. The peaks matched the days Chloe's Book Club had met, and that returned his thought to her. The rent from next door was helping the bottom line, but that was a temporary fix, and brought his thoughts back to Kennedy. He tossed the pen onto the desk and closed the tabs on his computer.

The brisk morning air revived him somewhat, at least giving him something else to think about, and he managed to put a pleasant look on his face as he entered the Pot & Flagon. The Gossip Club was in full form, and he bought his coffee and bear claw without attracting their attention.

For nearly a minute.

"Well, Mr. Lennox, what do you have to add?"

"Miss Cobb, I just now arrived. What is our topic this morning?" From either side Sammi giggled and Maggie sighed.

"Kennedy Phillips's job status of course." Mary Jane spoke as if everyone knew and he should too. "You remember her, your tenant?"

This time Maggie giggled softly and Sammi sighed. "I'm sure she'll stay on through the election in November if Rassmussen wins," he said.

When the table collectively gasped at his woefully male ignorance, Gena said, "After last night's goings on, she may not have a candidate to back."

"The donor event at the Club?" Chris looked around the table. "Her dad wrote him a check, didn't he?"

Mary Jane held her finger and thumb an inch apart. "A teensy-weensy check."

He wondered how they could possibly know what had happened a scant twelve hours ago. No one at the table had been on the guest list. "Rassmussen must have expected more than that."

"A lot more." Gena glanced at the women to her left. "Gerri you know, works at the *Bugle*."

"But I'm not allowed to talk about it until the paper comes out."

Gena patted the older woman's hand.

"That's the only reason she got the job in the first place," Mrs. Morse said. The oval table in the bay window of the coffee shop agreed. "She was the key to her Daddy's bank account."

Chris faced them. "Since you know all this, do you know what the reason was? I thought her dad was pretty high on Rassmussen."

Teddi cleared her throat. "We didn't hear his speech, but we believe he never stated his position." Geraldine nodded quickly.

"On the book banning." The words burst from Morse's ferret-like face. Teddi nodded and continued. "I know that had been bothering Kennedy for several weeks."

The table quietly digested that until Mary Jane said, "She cut off her nose to spite her face."

"She had a responsibility to support her employer," Gena said. "He's the candidate, not her."

"It's not her money, it's her father's. Or the insurance company's." Chris' words caused another incredulous and short pause.

"And now he's probably going to lose, and she'll quit."

Gena nodded to Mary Jane and added, "I bet she already has quit. She won't stay in Benton Center after he loses."

"Remember the controversy over the homecoming queen election?" Sammi patted her Maggie's hand. "You should have won."

Chris didn't know what that had to do with anything. He raised both hands. "Yeah, I remember that, and there was something weird about her quitting the soccer team." The table murmured and he spoke over them. "But come on, that was what, nine years ago? Ten?"

"She still thinks she's better than everybody." Gena's voice was low. "Always will."

"I think she's more focused. You know, motivated? Like she's on a mission?" Mary Jane pitched the idea with her hands.

"No, she's still Miss All About Me." Gena said. "See, we're talking about her, not about the issues or even about the candidate." Many heads bobbed in agreement.

After several seconds, Teddi said quietly, "Do you think she has changed, Chris?"

He looked at the kind and reasonable barista across the table. "I don't know, she's different, I think. I mean she still dresses well and projects herself, but I don't know, I—"

"We can ask her." Sammi rose halfway and waved. Chris slid his chair closer to Maggie.

Kennedy stepped to the table and put her hands on her hips. "You guys been talking about me?" She was dressed in serious business attire. No one responded.

She settled onto the chair next to Chris. Her smile exposed her perfect white teeth and emphasized the contours of her cheeks. "Fire away."

No one spoke. Several averted their eyes "OK, I'll start. You already know the basic facts."

"I don't."

"No, Chris, you are not on the Ladies email chain."

"You sent that message?" Gena's voice rose sharply. "Why would you?"

"So you get the real information." Kennedy continued. "Here's some more.

"Anybody can run a campaign with a good candidate. It's easy. You get him to say the right things on the right platforms and off you go."

The women listened intently. Chris, too.

"I will make my mark in this industry by promoting a weak candidate. The Rassmussen for Senate office will remain open."

"You're not quitting?"

"No, Mary Jane, I am not. I signed a contract with the Rassmussen campaign, and I will honor that commitment."

"You'll lose the election. No way he carries this county."

"That may be, Ms. Cobb, but if so, I will go down fighting, guns blazing." Kennedy stared around the table. "That's what my father taught me."

No one spoke. "No more questions?"

Kennedy pushed away from the table. "I got work to do, thanks for the chat," she said and strode out of the Pot & Flagon.

Maybe she has changed, Chris thought. At least she'll keep paying the rent a while longer.

Chapter 31

The door tinkled behind her, either heralding her successful escape from the wagging tongues of the Gossip Club or the Ladies following her out of the coffee shop. Kennedy wasn't sure, but she did manage to slow her pace and steady her breathing before she reached the campaign HQ.

At least the lights were still on in her half of the bookshop building. She took another cleansing breath and straightened her suit before opening the door. "Alvin, still going strong," she said cheerfully as she entered.

"Living the dream, boss." He kept his face to the screen and raised his hand as she passed. "Rassy rules."

She high fived his palm and walked briskly to her office. Two volunteers were waiting for her, Sally and Denise or Dianne. She always got the two confused.

Sally held up a sheaf of door-to-door street maps. "Denise isn't coming, so we can't do all these." Dianne nodded beside her.

Kennedy set her Coach bag on her desk. "We'll just

do as many as we can today. Do we have enough literature?"

"Plenty of that," Sally replied. "Tons of it."

"That's good. Take as much as you need then." Kennedy smiled at the two, thinking that printed material in the office meant it wasn't being put in voters' hands. "Thanks for all your good work."

As the young women picked up flyers and maps and turned to go, Kennedy said, "What's up with Denise? Is she sick?"

"Working at the other HQ in Hartfield."

"Transferred," Dianne added.

"That's right," Kennedy said, and waved. No one had told her there was a campaign office in the neighboring county. Whatever, she thought. She knew Brenda would gladly undermine her, but Scott? He must be still smoldering from her father's donation.

She took another deep breath. No one said it would be easy. "Hold down the fort, Alvin." She slapped his palm again as she passed. "You're in charge."

"Yes, ma'am," he said with a grin.

The *Benton Center Bugle* was housed in a two-story stone building that fronted the Square. It ran back deeper than its neighbors and originally housed the presses as well as the editorial offices. The paper was now printed off-site. Kennedy climbed the wide, steep steps and admired the massive gray stone porch. *The Bugle* in ornate gold letters faced her in the window of the massive door. She pulled it open easily and entered.

"Is Mr. Montgomery in, Mrs. Flanagan?"

"Very formal, Ms. Phillips." The part-time Gossip Clubber must have raced from the coffee shop to beat her. "I'll check."

Kennedy admired the heavy dark molding and trim of the 150-year-old building as Flanagan spoke on the phone.

"Go on up," the receptionist said with a wave.

"Thanks, Gerri," Kennedy said and mounted the wide, twisting staircase.

The steps were shallow, and the railing fit easily into her hand. Kennedy knew people were shorter when the staircase was built; in more recent buildings she had to bend her elbow and reach up. Kennedy was thinking about architecture instead of her meeting with the editor.

Travis Montgomery was the third member of his family to manage the *Bugle*, and like the others, a no-nonsense stickler. He was standing in front of his desk and reached out his hand as she entered. "Miss Phillips. Nice to see you again." He stood nearly a foot taller than she, wearing a vest over his white shirt and tie and his trademark white handlebar moustache over his lip.

Kennedy gave his hand a firm squeeze. "My pleasure, Mr. Montgomery."

"Please. Monty." He ushered her to a high-backed, brass-studded leather chair and moved smoothly around his desk. "How's your dad?"

Not two minutes in the office, and he's talking about my father. She smiled brightly. "Wonderful."

"Glad to hear it, Kennedy, now what can I do for you?"

She didn't know when she changed from Miss Phillips to her first name, but at least he hadn't called her KK. "I'm here about the campaign, the Rassmussen campaign."

Montgomery's eyebrows raised in parallel with his moustache. "Is he still running?"

As the gunslinger he resembled, he fired first. Kennedy smiled. "Of course. Why would you think otherwise?"

"I was at the Country Club the other night."

"Then you know my father is supporting his campaign."

"With a paltry little check." He sighted his gaze at her and locked it in.

She increased the amplitude of her smile. "You have no idea the amount of the check."

"I don't?"

"No." She kept smiling and widened her eyes.

He blinked. "What I hear—"

"Hearing is not seeing, is it, Mr. Montgomery?"

"Monty, but, yes, everybody is—"

Kennedy fired, "Everybody is wrong. The *Bugle* deals in facts traditionally, not in gossip."

He couldn't find the words. "Yes, but—"

She stood up. "The Rassmussen campaign is still alive in Benton Center. I am still in charge of the county HQ."

At the door, she said, "Thank you for your time, Mr. Montgomery."

The editor leaned back in his chair as she closed it. She was the spitting image of her father. And her grandfather, for that matter. He slapped the top of his desk and smiled.

Kennedy smiled to herself as she clacked her heels down the stone steps of the newspaper office and thanked her father. It was only a skirmish, but she had won and hopefully had bought herself some time. The *Bugle* was the only paper in town, but it was a weekly and couldn't return her fire for several days. Or find answers to her deception.

Her satisfaction was short-lived. The lights were still on when she returned to the HQ, but no one was there. At Alvin's desk was a hastily scrawled note. "Kennedy, transferred to Hartfield office. Great working with you. Al-dog. PS, you could have told me! LOL!"

She slumped down into his office chair. Transferred by Brenda. Of course. Sorry Alvin, but I couldn't tell you what I didn't know.

She sighed and reached for her phone. Text from Sally: "Promoted to the new office in Hartfield. Me and both the D's together again! See you at the next regional staff meeting."

All my staff. Probably my funding, too. Kennedy looked around the vacant room. A light flashed on the office landline. As she stood to answer it, she realized she couldn't afford the BNB.

Chapter 32

It wasn't until several days later that Chris noticed the lack of activity in the campaign office next door. Buried in trying to keep the bookshop afloat, he would have missed even that if not for Chloe.

"Looks like Ms. Phillips needs a hug," she'd said.

"Don't worry," he'd replied. "I'm sure her father can buy her one."

"That's mean. Especially for my funcle."

"I'm not feeling very fun." He snapped the cover of his laptop shut to hide the numbers on his bank statement. "Aren't you supposed to be working the floor?"

"I can hear the door open from here." Chloe rearranged her legs in the chair. "It looks like no one is working there anymore. Most of the time, she's not there herself."

"They used to have a bunch of people, Alvin and all those volunteers." Chris didn't look up when he spoke.

"Simon and Theodore too." When Chris didn't

respond, Chloe pointed to the computer. "The numbers are bad?"

"Bad would be an improvement." He kept his eyes away from hers as if he could hide.

"I sold a couple books today," the teenager said hopefully.

"You're my best salesman."

"I'm your only salesman." That usually made him laugh, but this time it didn't.

"I didn't sell a single one today." He brought his eyes to hers. "Had two people pull a book from the shelf, read the blurbs, then pull out their phones and order it from Amazon. That really makes me mad."

She waited several seconds before saying, "Had a couple of them myself, but I didn't want to mention it."

He forced himself to smile. "You know I really appreciate you helping around here. You have no idea."

"Unc, we're family. Of course I'm helping." She squinted in the dim light of the office. "Besides, you're still paying me, right?"

He grinned at her change of emotion, not at his financial condition. "You, I'm paying. Me, that's another story." He held up his hand to ward off her concern. "If it gets really bad, you know I can sell out."

"Don't do that, it's been in the family for years."

"I know, but at least it's a safety net." Chris nodded toward the HQ. "I was kidding before about the hug, but she can ask dad to write a check and keep the doors open."

"She's not going to do that."

Chris looked up. "How do you know that?"

"I spoke to her a couple days ago." Chloe saw the expression on his face. "She doesn't bite, you know."

"She doesn't talk to me."

"You should give her a chance." Her uncle didn't

reply, and she said, "She's doing it on her own. No money from Dad, no help from the campaign. She's doing the canvassing, writing press releases and ads. Everything, by herself."

"Doesn't sound like her. At all."

Chloe glared. "Again, give her a chance. I don't even know where she's sleeping."

"She can go home to sleep. She's had more chances than most people." He shook his head. "She could at least pay the rent she owes us."

"That's so unfair!"

"Chloe, I know her, you don't."

"You knew her ten years ago. It's not her fault her family is rich."

"And it's not our fault our family is circling the drain either."

Chloe stood up in front of him. "Our family is not failing; our family business is failing. That's different."

Chris shook his head and forced a laugh. "Sit down, sit down, Chlo. You are the last person in the world I want to argue with."

"And your only salesman."

"My entire staff." He nodded. "You got any ideas? I'm fresh out."

"I don't know if it's an actual idea."

He opened his palms. "Better than anything I got."

"OK, look, so Rassmussen has pulled out and left Kennedy on her own, right?"

Chris nodded.

"How has she responded? She didn't quit. She didn't go running home to her father either."

Chris leaned his forearms on the desk. "What are you saying?"

"We should do what she's doing. Keep fighting."

"But we don't know what to do."

Chloe snatched the letter from BazillionBooks off his desk. "Well, we know this isn't the answer, is it?"

"The only one we got."

"No, the only one we got right now."

"Go on." He offered his upturned palm.

"There is no way Kennedy can do all the work of the campaign in the entire county, right?"

Chris nodded.

"So what is she doing? Going door to door in the mornings and setting up a table in the Square afternoons. Is it enough to win? Probably not, but she's putting herself out there. Everybody has seen her. I'm sure she has gotten some votes."

"Where are you going with this?" He watched her hands fly around as she thought.

"What do we want? Keep the bookshop, right?"

"Right. Sell more books."

"And what one thing is stopping us from doing that? Not the national trends, the internet or stuff like that. Locally. What is hurting us locally?"

"The book banning thing. The controversy."

"Yes, so what can we do about that?"

"The Board of Education is going to decide. Nothing, I guess."

"Uncle Chris, you're not listening! Did Kennedy stop when everyone pulled out on her?"

"No, I—"

"She didn't. She stood up and is doing the few things she can."

Chris's eyes narrowed, then his face opened. "We can take a position against book banning."

"In a place where we can't be shouted down like you were at the demonstration."

"The newspaper. We'll take out an ad in the *Bugle*."

"It may not work—" Chloe began.

"—but we'll be taking a shot," Chris finished.

Chapter 33

It's kind of a cliché, but most small towns in the Midwest love festivals. The Christmas festival with tree-lighting, Santa's appearance and of course, a parade is a staple. Fall festivals, spring festivals, festivals dedicated to local businesses like candles and bees and matchsticks, and festivals honoring bratwurst, broccoli and garlic dot the calendars in small-town Middle America. Everyone loves to get together and celebrate. Benton Center, Ohio, is no exception: its PumpkinFest is among the most popular in the state.

Beyond the celebration, beyond the music, the food, the games, the camaraderie and the fun is where Benton Center is exceptional: their festivals are centered around democracy. The essence of democracy in this small town is voting, and their festivals take place around election days. PumpkinFest with its Halloween theme is always the weekend before election day in November, and VotersFest is the weekend before the May primary. If there is a special election, a festival will spring up spontaneously. It's in the town's DNA.

What does democracy have to do with a good party? The people of Benton Center probably would answer that in many different ways, and maybe that's the point: everyone has an opinion, and sharing diverse opinions is the essence of this community. The key to all this is the civility of the discourse, and that's how VoterFest started long ago.

In the midst of an extremely heated discussion, maybe even an argument, about tax money being used for snow removal, one side paused and delivered hot chocolate and warm sticky buns to the other side. At least that's one of the many versions a visitor could hear on the sidewalks of Ben Cen or in the Pot & Flagon.

This year's issue, of course, was centered on whether *Green Eggs and Ham* should be removed from the elementary school library. The issue itself would not appear on the May ballot, as the Board of Education would decide the matter later in the week. But the issue was present in many of the 10-by-10 pop up tents that lined the spokes of sidewalks radiating from the gazebo in the Town Square.

Mr. Morse and his wife Gladys had a tent promoting the banning of the book in question and other books as well. The senatorial candidates, Harvey and Rassmussen had tents. Groups supporting issues for the November election had tents with information. School board candidates had tents, vendors like Chris had tents, the mayor had a tent, the councilmen had tents and the library did as well. The Republicans and Democrats had tents, but the Independent Voters of Conway County's tent was much larger than both of them combined.

Then there were the food tents lining the sidewalks and parked along the curbs: local breweries, the wine bar, the hot dog place, the Yoder/Patel cookie shop, and, of course, the Pot & Flagon had its own tent where Teddi held court. Since his triumphant return last year, local folk singer Terry McGrath and his music students were entertaining the crowd from the gazebo stage.

Kennedy reached into the box underneath the table in the Rassmussen for Senate campaign tent. The box was nearly empty, reflecting her intensity level. As usual, she'd had trouble finding volunteers to help. She stretched her back and fanned the flyers across the red, white, and blue tablecloth. She'd promised herself to work the entire campaign alone if she had to.

"Rassmussen for Senate." She held out a flyer to a woman passing by. The woman looked away and didn't stop.

"Rassmussen for Senate," she said to an older couple.

"He still running?" the man said. "Thought he quit."

"He's in it to win it, sir." Kennedy smiled brightly. The man ignored her.

Kennedy grabbed a handful of the campaign literature and stepped around the table onto the sidewalk. She was harder to ignore and managed to hand out a dozen or so. A tall man walked through the crowd directly to her and asked for a flyer.

Kennedy looked up. "Oh, Mr. Montgomery, I didn't see you."

The *Bugle* editor grinned beneath his trademark moustache. "Politics is such a rewarding enterprise, is it not, Miss Phillips?"

"No, sir, at the grassroots level it is not."

He tapped the flyer in his palm and noticed the nearly empty tent. "Yet you carry on."

She forced a flyer into the hand of an elderly woman. "I made a promise, and I am keeping it. "Thank you, ma'am." Turning back to Montgomery, she said, "Thank you for your editorial. It helped."

"I didn't write it to help you, Miss Phillips, or the

Rassmussen campaign. I barely know the man."

Kennedy nodded and tried to hand a voter the flyer. "That's been our problem all along."

"It surely has locally," the editor agreed. "But the broader issue is big money in politics. It overwhelms the voters."

"I agree." Kennedy laid the stack of literature on the table and looked up at him. "But by focusing your piece on the voters instead on of the money, you let people know my father's position without stating it."

Montgomery nodded. "It's all about letting the people decide."

She smiled. "I appreciate it, Mr. Montgomery."

"I appreciate the job you're doing all by yourself." Over his shoulder he added, "Please. I've known you since you were a little girl. Call me Monty."

Several tents closer to the gazebo along the same path, Chris was trying to keep his temper in check and sell a few books while debating book banning with the Morses. "But there is no sexually explicit content in the book," he said.

"Explicit sexual content has no place in children's books," Mr. Morse said. Behind him, his pinch-faced wife nodded vigorously.

"Then we are in agreement." Chris handed change to a customer. "Thank you, ma'am."

"The language is offensive. Too much rhyming."

"Kids love rhyming, Mr. Morse."

"It's boring, Sam, ham, I am."

"Mrs. Morse, repetition makes it easier for the kids to read. It's a literary device." Chris watched several people stop, notice the Morse's, and walk away.

Mr. Morse pushed himself in front of his wife. "We're parents, we have the right to decide what our children are exposed to."

Chris nodded. "Of course you do. That's not the issue. What you don't have is the right to decide what other parents want their kids to read."

"But—"

"If you ban it, no one can read it." Chris stood up straight. "Now, if you'll excuse me, I'm trying to sell some books here."

"Oh, so that's it, isn't it." Mrs. Morse raised her voice and turned to the crowd. "Mr. Bookseller wants to sell books. No wonder he's *against* parents' rights!"

"No, I'm *for reading!*" Chris's hands balled into fists, but before he could act, Mayor Grieselhuber and several councilmen appeared and ushered the Morses away.

The crowd thinned and a soft voice said, "Thank you, Mr. Lennox." Joanie Kimble smiled shyly. "For standing up for what is right."

The second-grade teacher was small and dark-haired with sparkling brown eyes. She smiled again. "I really appreciate it."

"Hey, I'm not doing it for you, I'm just a capitalist."

Joanie clapped her hands excitedly. "No, you're not, you just need a break." She looked at him closely. "Take a walk?"

"Can't leave the tent. They'll steal my books. Or burn them." Chris looked up and down the sidewalk. "Wait, here's Chloe."

His cousin and her friend Cathy agreed to watch the booth, and he accompanied Joanie down the path.

Chapter 34

"*Buy you a* cookie?" Joanie grinned. They stopped at Patel and Yoder's cookies. Sammi, her mother and her mother-in-law baked traditional Amish and Indian sweets.

"They're free, you know," Chris said.

"If you're a voter!" Sammi held up a plate in either hand. "I know you guys vote, so take one. Or two!"

Chris and the teacher munched their treats and continued flowing with the crowd. "I loved your ad in the *Bugle*," she said. "Right on point."

"Thanks, I don't know if it will help, but I had to say it."

"It was clear, for sure." Joanie stopped. "*Why I love reading and hate banning.* Thanks for doing that."

"I'm glad I did. So many people—you saw them—think I'm in it for the money. I'm not totally, but I have to stay afloat. Keep the store open."

"You will, Chris," She laid her hand on his arm, then pulled if off to wave. "Maggie!" She ran through the crowd toward the gazebo, and he followed.

On stage, Maggie's father Terry and her husband Brent were leading their young music students through The Byrds' version of "Turn, Turn, Turn." Mary Jane's daughter, Meredith, and Teddi's nephew, Petey, were also part of the music class. Joanie and Maggie hugged.

When the song ended, Chris raised an atta-boy fist to Brent and thanked Joanie for the cookie. "Gotta get back to the tent."

She squeezed his hand, and he stepped back into the flow of happy voters.

Gena stepped in front of him as he passed the Benton Center tent and thrust a clipboard into his hands. "Fill this out." She found a woman in the crowd and accosted her in the same manner.

Chris looked at the one-page form. It was a survey from the city regarding traffic lights. Where to put them, how to time them, and whether they were needed or not. He quickly filled in the circles and looked for Gena. The mayor's secretary was working the crowd, not standing behind the table in the tent. Every so often, she would return to the tent and drop pennies into one of two glass jars.

"Here's your survey, Gena." She took it from him, put a fresh sheet on top and jammed it into the hands of a passerby.

"Thank you for your input," she said without looking at him.

When she turned to find her next victim, he said, "What's with the pennies?"

"None of your business." She scanned the crowd and didn't meet his eyes.

"Looks like your own little survey."

Her face appeared in front of his. "No, it isn't."

"It sure looks like it. You put a penny for me in the

left jar and a penny for the book banners in the other one. You're taking a straw vote on the book issue."

"Don't tell anybody," she hissed.

"My lips are sealed."

She stared at him full in the face. "You better not."

"Or what, you're going to put me out of business?" Before she could retort, he added, "I don't need any help doing that myself."

Gena turned away and Chris continued around the other side of the gazebo. One of the kids on stage was doing a guitar solo or choking a cat; it was hard to tell. A large crowd blocked the path ahead of him and he stopped to listen.

Mike Harvey, Rassmussen's opponent in the senatorial race, was speaking through a megaphone. "That's why, ladies and gentlemen, I refuse to pay for books that disrespect your values, our values, and the values of Benton Center and Conway County."

Several people clapped. The crowd pressed forward.

"Surveys have shown that when kids are exposed to violence, they become more violent. When they are exposed to sexual content—"

Chris didn't need to hear any more. He left the crowd and cut across the grass to the next spoke of sidewalk. It was quieter here, the music faded and the applause thankfully faint. He sat on an empty bench and noticed the tent opposite.

Kennedy sat motionless on a folding chair behind the table in the Rassmussen tent. No one was there with her, and no one was interested in the literature or the candidate. He felt sorry for her.

Teddi suddenly appeared on the bench next to him. "Girl needs a friend."

"What?"

"You been staring at her for a quarter hour, young man. I watched you from my perch." She indicated the P & F tent with her thumb. "Follow me." He did.

The coffee shop tent was larger than the others, with tables and space for two dozen people. It was half full as Teddi slid two paper cups across the counter. "This one, the one on your left, is what she wants."

Chris furrowed his brow. "There's like four lines of dialogue on her cup. Mine just says 'whole'."

"She's picky. As if you didn't know that." Teddi's teeth flashed in the dim light. "Just give it to her; say it's from me."

Chris picked up the cups and started for the exit of the tent.

"Or you could say it was from you." Teddi arched her eyebrows.

Chris was puzzled at the barista's tone. Why would he be giving Kennedy of all people a latte? Why would Kennedy accept a latte from him?

Kennedy snapped, "Are you here for the rent?" and locked her arms around herself. "I told you I'd pay."

"You did." Chris set her cup on the table and took a sip from his own. Her nails were jagged, the polish chipped.

She dropped her hands to her sides. "But here you are harassing me."

"I'm just standing here drinking my latte." He savored a sip. "I know you'll pay. I'll be out of business by then, but you'll pay when you get around to it."

"All about you, is it?" She snorted a breath and grabbed for the latte without looking at it. "It's hot!" She slammed the cup onto the table, and hot coffee sloshed out onto the stack of literature.

He laughed without thinking. "Ooopsie!"

"You made me ruin it, the whole stack!" Her eyes

bugged out, her cheeks reddened, her breath sped up. "It's your fault."

Chris carefully set his cup down and slowly stepped back. He didn't know what she would do.

She laughed. He checked to see if she was gagging or choking. No, she was laughing. But her eyes were red and watery. Her hair wild, strands flying askew, others stuck to her forehead.

"Like anybody's gonna read it!" Her voice was high-pitched and screechy, her face maniacal. "I can't give this crap away!"

He had never seen her this way. "Are you—"

"Nobody cares about Scotty Rassy, no one!" She grabbed her cup and poured the rest of it over the other stacks of paperwork. "So what if I ruin it!"

Chris reached for his cup, but she turned her shoulder into him and snatched it before he could. She tore off the plastic lid and poured the hot liquid into the box of literature on the floor. "There. Now no one can read *any* of it."

She whirled toward him and extended her arms. "It doesn't say *any*thing *any*way. It's all fluff and smiles. Not one word about what he believes or what his positions are."

Without thinking he opened his arms to embrace her. "Kennedy, I'm sorry—"

The rest of what Chris was about to say was lost as Kennedy reached up on her tip toes and kissed him full on the mouth. Before he could pull his thoughts together or say a word, she had fled the tent and disappeared into the crowd.

Chapter 35

Chris tried telling himself he was a creature of habit. Obviously, everyone in Benton Center knew about it, it had happened almost twelve hours ago, so he was sure to be taken to task by the ladies if he dared to enter the Pot & Flagon. He was certainly confused by her kiss but also a little bit proud; he had dreamed about it as a boy. Besides, he told himself, it probably meant nothing to her, and a bear claw and mocha latte really were his morning habit.

He changed his mind immediately and froze in the doorway. Kennedy was at the table with the Gossip Club and only a fool would join them. He slunk to the counter and kept his back to the ladies. Minutes later he was safely back in the bookshop, pulling the sweet pastry from the paper sack and berating himself for not being bolder.

He must have dozed off. He jumped when the door opened and Sammi appeared. "First customer of the day," he managed as he got to his feet.

She plopped down on the chair opposite and took

in the small table and chairs and pile of toys. "I can't wait till I have my baby and we can come to reading club here."

He sat back down. "Assuming we're still open."

"Don't be such a Gloomy Gus. What does Rick call you, Derrick Downer? Of course you'll still be open."

She nodded and smiled so enthusiastically that Chris found himself following suit. "OK, you win. Are you looking for something specific?"

"Not today." Sammi looked side to side as if she were about to share a secret. "Kennedy visited me last night. At the Dress Shop."

Chris nodded. He had no idea what to say.

"She has been in the Dress Shop one time in her entire life, Chris. Once."

"Not the coolest place in town, so, OK, I get it. What was the occasion?"

"You, Christopher Lennox. You were the occasion." Sammi sat back and beamed.

"What? I—oh no." He thought for a moment. "Last time I saw her she was racing out of the tent."

"She came straight to the shop, shut the door behind her and dropped onto the sofa. My mother nearly fainted."

"Like I was chasing her."

The smile faded on Sammi's face. "No—well, my mother brought us tea and we sat and talked for almost an hour. The longest I ever talked with her." She looked away. "I think she was chasing herself."

Chris glanced at the Square where the Rassmussen tent had stood, then back at the nicest person in Ben Cen. "I have no idea what that means."

"She's embarrassed."

"She's embarrassed that she kissed me? Great."

"No, no not that." Sammi leaned forward. "She's

embarrassed that she lost control and trashed the campaign literature."

"And kissed me."

"No, that's not what I mean." Sammi's hands fluttered before settling on her rounded stomach.

"Then what?" Chris took a breath and tried to focus. "She freaked out, lost control whatever, and part of that was kissing me?"

"Look, Chris, be nice to her. She's fragile." Sammi's eyes widened.

"Right. Kennedy is as fragile as a hockey puck."

"I knew you'd say something like that." Sammi's golden brown face tightened in a frown. "Like Teddi was saying this morning. She's always felt the pressure from her father to do everything right. She's supposed to be perfect. Expected to be."

"You're saying kissing me is an imperfection. Something beneath her." That was how she had always treated him. The few times she even noticed him.

"No, Chris, but she's hurting inside."

He waved his arms to include the bookshop, and his voice rose. "I'm hurting too."

"She's trying, but she's going to lose the primary election. That's on her."

"I'm trying, and I'm losing my family's bookshop."

"See, you have a lot in common." Sammi raised a hopeful smile.

"Samantha, you're the most positive person I know. Maybe the most positive person in town. But you are stark raving nuts. Kennedy Phillips does not know who I am. She barely knows I exist."

She gave him a second. "What do you really know about her?'

"I know all I need to know about her."

"Beyond her beautiful exterior?"

"You mean her flawless, impenetrable shell?" He clasped his hands. "Sammi, I felt sorry for her yesterday. Working alone in her booth. No staff to help. I really did feel sorry for her, and she accused me of harassing her for the rent money. And ran away." He shook his head. "I got enough problems of my own. I don't need any more."

Several storefronts east of where Chris and Sammi were talking, the Ladies Gossip Club was recounting an extremely interesting morning. It was now after ten, the morning rush was over, and Teddi had joined the table.

"It's like they just paraded in here one at a time," Mary Jane was saying.

"Chris hardly paraded," Gena said. "He skulked in and out of here and pretended we couldn't see him. Like an ostrich."

Mary Jane pursed her lips. "My point was, both of them were here separately."

"I didn't think either of them would show. Not after yesterday's display." Maggie wiped the last bit of sugar from her lips. "That was embarrassing."

"What did you think about Kennedy denying it even happened?" Gena gestured with half of a chocolate covered cream stick. "She said she never kissed him."

"No one was in the tent to see it." Teddi set down her heavy mug. As if the town itself had eyes.

"But we all know it, Theodora, come on." Mary Jane dismissed the idea with a wave of her hand. "Besides it wasn't really a tent; it didn't have sides."

"We have been known to misunderstand the facts." Teddi shook her head in response. "That's what I'm saying."

Mary Jane continued as if Teddi hadn't spoken. "Besides she still thinks Rassmussen can pull it off. She's denying everything."

"Her candidate is going to lose the primary," the pinch-faced Mrs. Morse said. "If the book banning issue were on the ballot, it would pass. Either way, the young man will lose the bookstore."

The table sat quietly for a moment, digesting her message along with their donuts. Teddi tapped the newspaper lying open before her. "The thing of it is, both the young people will probably lose, as Gladys pointed out, but they're both hanging in there. Look at this week's *Bugle*. They haven't quit."

"Her daddy will not be happy," Gena said.

"His family has owned that store for generations."

Teddi nodded. "That's why I think Kennedy is denying it, and Chris would, too, if we asked him. Neither one wants to let down their family."

Chapter 36

It was cold in the HQ side of the bookstore. Colder than it was outside, Chris thought as he crossed from his side into hers. Quieter, too. When the campaign had been going full force, the place had nearly throbbed with activity. Phones ringing, people coming and going with a tension generated by volunteers pulling together toward a common goal.

Chris pulled the door shut behind him and it was quieter still. Kennedy was facing a computer screen away from him. He knocked his knuckles on the door jam. She didn't move.

"Hello. You've got company." He lifted his voice with as much cheer as he could manage. Despite Sammi's exhortation, there was only so much he was capable of.

Kennedy kept her face to the computer and waved a hand. Apparently he was to wait for her attention. I just want to know why she kissed me, he thought.

"Leave the mail on the table there, please." She kept typing, hoping he would go away. "Thank you."

"Not the mail man," Chris said.

Kennedy turned around. "Oh."

"Oh, I can't wait to kiss him again? Or oh, time to run away again?"

The last thing I need is him, she thought. This morning was enough. She turned back to the screen. "I don't know what you're talking about."

"Yesterday, at the VotersFest, you—" He stopped speaking and faced her above the computer screen. "You know what you did. I want to know why."

"No idea what you're talking about." She typed harder, mashing the keys with her fingers.

"Yes, you do and so does Benton Center."

She looked up. "Never happened."

"You kissed me."

"Nope."

"And you ran away."

"No way." Her fingers flew across the keyboard. She had no idea what she was typing. If he would only leave!

"That's what Sammi told me." He grinned as she flinched at the woman's name. "I was there, too, I know what happened."

I didn't think she'd spill the beans so fast, Kennedy thought. She stopped typing and looked at him hovering over the screen of the desktop. "I was rattled. There, are you happy now? I admitted I was rattled. Upset."

He grinned at her defiant demeanor. "Rattled about the kiss or rattled about running away?"

"Both," she blurted. "Neither. All the above."

"Wait. You, Kennedy Phillips, the person who is never the slave to her emotions—"

"Yes. Yes to all of it." She rolled her chair away from the computer and from him.

"You're actually admitting that?" Chris gathered his

eyebrows. Kennedy sharing a weakness had to be a trick.

"Yes, I let myself go. I was overcome. I was Passion's Plaything." She focused her glare on him. "Now, will you please leave?"

He didn't move. "And it embarrassed you?"

"I'm not like that." She stood up. "Is that enough?"

He grinned. "What embarrassed you more, the kiss or trashing the campaign literature or running away?"

"The kiss." She saw the pain flash across his face and added, "Obviously."

Chris rallied. "OK, then, we're back to your normal behavior."

She didn't know what to say. He took another swing. "I thought for a moment there you might actually have liked me."

Ambushed, she thought. He snuck in here and attacked me. "Nope, I was rattled. As I mentioned several times already."

Chris watched her wrap her arms around herself. "That's the Kennedy we all know. Back in control."

She felt her cheeks redden. "So, if that's all you have?" She nodded toward the door.

"Oh, no I forgot to ask earlier. How's the campaign going? Rassy gonna win?"

"Don't worry, Chris, I've got the rent money."

"Not what I asked, but that's great. I'll be out of business by the time you pay anyway."

She watched him turn his face away in embarrassment. "The data shows that our lead has evaporated, we're trending downward, and we could lose by double digits."

He heard the life fade from her tone and watched her shoulders slump. When her eyes met his, he flashed the largest grin he could muster. "You're saying there's a chance!"

"No, no of course—" Curiosity replaced confusion, a smile began to form, and Kennedy blurted out a laugh, a hearty from deep inside laugh. Tears sprang from her eyes.

Chris joined in. "That's good to hear." He put his arms around her.

"I can't remember the last time I laughed." She stepped into his embrace.

"Wait." He felt her shoulders heave and stepped back. "None of that."

"You made me." She wiped snot from her nose. "You started it."

"No, you did." He handed her a tissue.

She dabbed her nose and her eyes. "But look, I didn't run away."

He noticed her wary smile. "Is there anything I can do to help you?" He waved vaguely at the empty room.

"No, but thank you." She smiled. "See, still not running away."

"This time."

"This time," she repeated. "But seriously, it's probably better if you stick to your side and I stick to mine."

"But we both need—" His words were blotted out by her cell phone. She turned away and jammed it to her ear. "Daddy. No, I have time."

Chris stepped away as she mouthed something to him while pressing the phone to her ear. He didn't look back as he left her space and returned to his side of the building. Besides, Chloe's Book Club was meeting this afternoon and he had to get her set up.

Chapter 37

It was tough for Chris to concentrate. The Board of Education was about to deliver its decision on the book banning issue. It was important to him personally, because he was against the concept of banning, and professionally, as the decision would greatly affect his business. Maybe even put him out of business.

But he couldn't put Kennedy out of his mind. Or her kiss, misguided or not. He puffed out his breath and looked around the Benton Center High School auditorium. It was many times larger than the normal meeting room in the Board building, and it was nearly full. He got up again to let people pass his seat on the aisle. He was uncomfortable despite the padded seats and wanted to be able to leave quickly.

Before he sat back down, he saw her enter the noisy, high-ceilinged room. Was she alone? Was that Maggie with her? Sammi? He felt exposed and embarrassed standing in the aisle and slunk down into his seat. He craned his head to find her, but she was swallowed up by the crowd.

He glanced at the time on his phone. Seven-fifteen, late getting started. Probably because they were confiscating signs and noisemakers at the door. Several board members were seated, but neither the superintendent nor the treasurer. He stood up again telling himself he was checking to see if the crowd was seated according to their positions on the issue, but he was hoping to see her. He thought they were both against the ban, but her kiss made him doubt everything he knew about her.

A microphone screeched and he startled like a nervous cat. Dianne Maybury tapped the instrument again and the room settled; Chris settled his breathing. "Let us stand for the Pledge." The crowd recited the words, and the meeting began. Chris scanned the crowd as he stood but didn't see her.

Kennedy could see him from her seat in the balcony. She couldn't not see him. Every time she tried to look at the stage, her eyes shifted to him. *Why had I kissed him?* she thought. *That's not me.* Maggie and Sammi were talking to each other across her, and she feigned interest in what they were saying, but she couldn't keep her eyes away from Chris. *It's like he can't sit still. He keeps squirming in his seat.*

Maybury handed the meeting over to Dr. Fine, who went on to describe the process leading to this meeting. The man's head was bald front to back, but bushy gray hair sprouted over his ears from the sides. He summarized the previous public meeting and the subsequent closed meetings. Chris couldn't concentrate enough to follow all the details but understood the main message. Because of all the discussions and consultations the board had held, they felt knowledgeable enough to simply express their decision. Tonight's meeting would be brief: in a representative democracy, the elected members of the Board of Education make the decisions.

Dr. Fine squinted at the crowd through his dark-rimmed glasses until it quieted back down. "We have decided to remove *Green Eggs and Ham* by Dr. Seuss from the school libraries." About half of the audience cheered, the other half booed and whistled. I'm out of business, Chris thought. He searched for her again but didn't find her.

"In addition," Dr. Fine said, "we have decided to set up a committee to further examine this issue, and recommend further action, if it is warranted." It appeared that different people cheered and booed this time. Chris didn't much care: it was just more people who hadn't read the book putting in their two cents. "This committee will also take a look at textbooks currently in use and make recommendations regarding them if necessary."

The crowd reacted to this along the same lines. Pros and cons, cheering and booing. Chris got up and joined a trickle of people heading for the exits. The board president was explaining the composition of the committee, but he wasn't interested. All it meant was the book banners were winning, and he would have to sell the business. Or give it away. He held the door for an elderly couple and remembered Rick was working tonight. A couple beers wouldn't hurt if he could keep his friend from talking about Kennedy.

Kennedy watched him slink from the room, head down and hands in pocket. She wanted to talk to him, but he would be gone before she could descend the stairs and reach him. Besides, she didn't want to have to explain herself to Sammi and Maggie.

I can't explain myself to myself, she thought. I don't like him. I never liked him. I barely know him. She smiled and nodded at something Maggie was saying. But I kinda want to talk to him again. Sammi was reaching across her to talk to Maggie. She leaned back and smiled to the women again. *He looks like he needs someone to talk to.*

Chapter 38

The Ladies of Benton Center Gossip Club meetings were almost always morning affairs. Items were discussed in the light of day over coffee and homemade pastry. At the big oval table in the bay window of the coffee shop. In full view of the Square and the Gazebo and the people passing by.

Sometimes, however, the Ladies met at night. When affairs in the community were so important they could not be postponed until morning. Then the meetings were held in the rear of the coffee shop, in the Flagon side. Out of sight of the Square and the passersby. At a table pushed against the refurbished brick wall, far from the small window opening on the side street. In the storeroom of the former grocery store, where spirits were sold, not coffee.

That did not necessarily mean the agenda topics were clandestine or somehow unworthy of discussion in and of themselves. No, everything that happened in the small town was worthy; it's just that some things were too pressing to keep until morning.

It felt different at night in the Flagon. Kennedy peered through the window to be sure the Ladies were actually there before reaching for the door handle. Mondays were dark, but of course Teddi would have the key. She gathered herself to settle her fears, stepped up and opened the door. Everyone turned to look at her. Gena, Mary Jane, Mrs. Morse, Gerri, Sammi, and Maggie. Teddi indicated an open chair next to Joanie Kimble and Kennedy took it.

"I didn't know you'd be meeting, here. Tonight." Kennedy held her hands together to prevent them from flying about.

"But you got here." Gena's voice was flat, and Kennedy couldn't read her expression.

"I was just sort of wandering around. After the board meeting."

"Glad you made it." Teddi smiled, then nodded at Joanie. "You were saying, dear?"

The second-grade teacher took a breath. "They told me not to worry, but I don't have tenure and I am worried." She dropped her gaze to the wine glass in front of her. "About my job."

"But you didn't do anything wrong." Sammi looked around the table for confirmation.

Maggie nodded. "You certainly didn't start this whole thing."

"You're clearly in the middle of it." Gena's tone was non-committal, and Kennedy again couldn't read it.

Mary Jane looked away from the teacher. "They'll need to find a scapegoat."

"That's unfair." Kennedy was surprised by how quickly and sharply the words escaped her. When everyone looked at her, she wrangled her hands tighter together and said as calmly as she could, "All you're trying to do is get the kids to read something fun."

Joanie's face lit up. "Thank you. At least someone understands."

Gena shook her head. "Unfortunately, the controversy started in your classroom."

"Someone has to pay, and she's the easy target." Kennedy stood up. "I get it. Sounds like politics."

Joanie turned and looked up at her. "Maybe the committee will work."

"It could." Kennedy returned her hopeful smile. "Anyway, I have to get back to the HQ. Tomorrow's the election."

Mary Jane furrowed her brow. "Rassmussen have a chance?"

Kennedy arranged a smile on her face and said brightly, "You never know until the voters speak." She spun away before anybody could contradict her.

The door closed behind her, and Gena said, "The girl's deluded if she thinks he'll win."

The others agreed. Teddi did as well, adding, "But you have to give her credit. She's hanging in there, alone, at night."

They sat digesting that and drinking their wine until Sammi said, "Anyway, if she's deluded about anything, it's about the kiss."

"Sammi, you shouldn't—"

"Maggie, the Ladies need to know, and probably do anyway." Sammi looked at the faces around her, hoping that they didn't know, and she would get credit for bringing up this juicy tidbit.

"Give, Samantha, all the details," Mary Jane demanded. Teddi sighed.

Sammi took a breath and related the events on the Square from the end of the demonstration to their conversation in the Dress Shop.

"So, you didn't actually *see* the kiss." Gena cocked her head to the side.

"No, I wasn't there." Sammi opened her hands. "But who would make that up?"

"They hate each other," Maggie said. "They have for years. Since high school."

"*She* kissed *him?*" Mary Jane squinted as if she couldn't see across the table. "Not the other way around?"

"I couldn't believe it either. But that's what she said." Sammi pursed her lips. "Told my mother, too."

Teddi laughed. "No one can lie to your mother."

The others agreed. Maggie said, "I tried once, remember?"

Sammi giggled. "Came home late and you made up a story—"

"I tried to make up a story." Maggie leaned across the table, her face serious. "But one look from your mom, and hey, I just blurted out the truth."

"You got me grounded." The ladies laughed at the story and the look on Sammi's face.

When they settled, Teddi said, "We have established the truth of the kiss, am I correct?" When the others nodded, she continued, "Are you shocked?"

"Like Maggie said, they hate each other. Yes, I am shocked," Gena said. "Aren't you?"

The Black woman folded her hands in her lap. "No, I am not. I do believe I had an inkling."

"There's no way this is going anywhere." Mary Jane gestured with her glass of Moscato. "She didn't know he was alive."

The table agreed. Teddi nodded. "Yup, that's what she said, right? We've all heard her say that, time and again."

Sammi spoke when no one else did. "Then how can you say you saw it coming?"

Teddi grinned slightly. "As Shakespeare said—"

"No, no way can you quote the Bard!" Gena's voice rose in pitch and volume.

Teddi waited for silence and the eye contact of the gossip club. "Surely I can. Probably not the exact words, but along the lines of 'I think you protest too much'."

"Wait. What?"

Teddi's open palms drew them in. "Over and over she'd say, 'I don't know him, I didn't know he existed, he means nothing to me.'"

"And by that she meant the opposite? Come on, Theodora." Gena folded her arms across her chest.

"What it meant is that he bothered her. He got under her skin."

Sammi nodded vigorously. "Yes, so she went out of her way to ignore him."

"Yes, she could say that. She worked to ignore him but couldn't get him out of her mind."

"She's a damn good actress."

"Well, she is, but it's like an irritation, an itch that Kennedy could never quite shake." Teddi looked around the table. "Why else in the world would she come back to Benton Center? She'd made her escape."

"Her father's money?" Mary Jane said. Others nodded.

"Maybe so." Teddi paused. "But I think it was time to scratch that itch."

Chapter 39

Chris took the long way back to the bookshop from the brew pub. The beers hadn't helped, but talking to Rick, listening really, had gotten him out of his head for a few minutes. At least he'd managed to keep the conversation on small business marketing, not his love life. He enjoyed walking in the quiet town, and the weather had been pleasant on the way from the board meeting. Now the farther he got from the pub, the cooler the night became. He raised the collar of his jacket and increased his pace. The weather was matching his mood.

His business was over. He'd have to close the bookshop. The sentences repeated themselves to match the tempo of his footsteps. The closer he got to his destination, the closer he was to financial ruin. He jumped as the car horn blared and he realized he was in the middle of the street. "Idiot!" the driver yelled, and he was forced to agree.

The wooden O's in the Lennox Family Bookshop sign glared down at him as he opened the door beneath them. Chloe had left the mail on his desk and closed the shop to attend the meeting. Just as well. His niece didn't need to see him in this condition.

He could wait to tell her the truth. Maybe it would work out for her; the new owners would probably like to keep her on. It was a hopeful thought, one that he didn't really believe, but it was better than the obvious. She could concentrate on her own life, not the wreck of his.

He hung his coat on the tree and grabbed the broom and dustpan. The front room was a mess after Chloe's last book club. He wasn't mad the girl hadn't cleaned, she was the pleasant face of the store. Not him. Besides, it was good to keep busy, he told himself, and actually accomplish something.

Unlike his bottom line. The book ban was a death knell. Sure, it was limited to the second grade and the elementary school library. For now. But the research showed that one book banned inevitably led to more books banned, and the scope would expand across the whole curriculum. Book sales would drop even farther. There would be exceptions and small groups that would read in spite of the rulings, but not enough to keep his business afloat.

He swept the last of the dirt into a smaller pile and scooped it into the dustpan. Walking through the stacks to the trash barrel, he remembered the stack of envelopes on the office desk. Only more bad news, he thought as he passed. Back at the counter in front, he picked up the rag and the spray can and reminded himself again that he should have dusted before he swept the floor. Maybe he really didn't deserve to own a business.

The Lennox Family Bookshop. His family. He was the last of his family and this was the last of the bookshop. In the back of his mind, he'd hoped that he could hold out long enough for Chloe to take over, but he didn't want to burden her with a losing proposition. No, he'd take the hit. He'd make the best deal he could and close the doors. He'd be the one to end the tradition.

He ran the cloth across the face of the huge brass cash register perched on the counter. He found a smudge on the glass, sprayed it again and stood back to make sure the big white letters were legible in their black frames. His grandfather had taught him to figure percentages on the ancient machine and he punched "No Sale" as the old man had when finished cleaning. The key receded a good two inches, gears ground, bells tinkled, and the white-on-black sign popped into the window. No matter what, he told himself, I won't sell it.

He tossed the rag onto the counter next to the cash register. No idea what I'll do with it, but no idea what I'll do for a job, either. Selling the family business doesn't have much resume value. He shook his head and somehow laughed. Now she kisses me, now she hugs me.

Perfect timing, he told himself. He set the spray can and cloth back on the shelf and retreated to his office. After all these years of ignoring me, now when I have no idea how to get my life on track, now when I can't get two coherent thoughts together, now she indicates she has feelings for me.

He dropped down into the soft leather of his office chair. It would be funny, hilarious even, if I were a big drinker. Or if I really were crazy. But no. I'm just an out of work, former bookseller. He rifled through the stack of letters, searching for the logo of BazillionBooks. He ripped open the envelope and skimmed to the third paragraph. There in black-on-white was the offer. The dated, one-time offer to buy the building, the books, and the name. One month to decide. It wasn't a lot, but more than he'd expected.

He dropped the letter and leaned back into the chair. It welcomed him and his eyes drifted.

He was sitting on his father's lap, in a big, high-backed chair. Behind them with a hand on the ornate curved frame stood his grandfather. The chair was red velvet, the wooden frame gilded. Grampa's beard and hair white, his father's black and his own slicked down and parted on the side. My Lennox Boys, his mother had called them.

Chris went around the desk and took the photograph down from its place beneath the big Regulator clock. Another thing he would never sell. His gaze fell to the photograph in his hands: These two men had taught him to cherish books. They had taught him to read. He would not let them down.

Chapter 40

Chris didn't know the Germans had a word for it, but his first reaction was clearly *Schadenfreude*: no matter how bad he was feeling at least he was up and walking and had a plan. A crummy plan, but as he peered into the HQ side of his building, better than whatever plan Kennedy had. She lay asleep in front of a computer, her head resting on the keyboard. He noticed several suitcases and a cardboard box on the floor at her feet. He hesitated, but the door was unlocked, and he entered.

The night before an election should be exciting, electric, vibrant. The Rassmussen Campaign office was lifeless, dark, cold. Even his failing bookstore had lights. How the mighty have fallen, he thought, and started to grin.

"Come here to gloat?" she said without turning her head.

"Sorry, I, uh, just wanted to see if you needed anything."

"Sure, you did." Kennedy stretched her back and brought her eyes to his face. It was the last person she wanted to see. "You're here to poke the bear."

Chris shrugged. "I'm not sure what that means."

Kennedy stood up. "You're just like all the other people in this town. You expected me to fail, and—" She swung her arm in a wide arc. "Boy, did I ever. You must be happy."

"Why would I be happy?"

Because you're one of them, she thought. Although he did look baffled. "They're calling me Loser Barbie, right?"

"I don't know. Does Loser Barbie get to wear pink, or does she have to do gray or beige?" He returned her glare. "OK, I get it, but the election's tomorrow, isn't it? There's time—"

"No, there isn't." Her arm dropped like an empty balloon, and she leaned over to pick up the cardboard box. "I'll be out of your hair as soon as I can."

If she leaves, he thought, one of my problems is solved. He tried to keep the smirk off his face. "Which was worse, losing the election or losing Rassy?"

The table shook as she slammed the box down next to the computer. "How dare you!"

He recognized her pain and wished he didn't enjoy it so much. "Wait, you weren't really in love with Rassy were you? You knew he was only after your family money, right?"

"He *was* in love with me!"

Same old KK. "Of course, he was. Everybody loves you."

She glared at him. "That's not true." At least I took a chance on love. That's more than you can say."

He softened his tone. "Right. How many times have you dumped a guy vs how many times have you been dumped?"

"OK, not many." She turned away from him and re-arranged the items in the box.

The polish on her nails was cracked and her hands trembled. He knew that feeling. "Now the shoe's on the other foot."

She closed the flaps on the box. "What makes you an expert on love?"

"Scars," he said. You should know, he thought.

Kennedy stood and faced him, the box clutched in her hands. "I should listen to a fellow loser, that's what you're saying?"

Chris nodded at the pillow and blanket on the sofa and the pizza boxes spilling out of the trash barrel. "Well, you're the one sleeping in an office and eating nutritious carry out."

She tried to step past him. "You're mean."

"That's another thing. Does anyone ever criticize you? Or are you so far up there that everyone down here on earth is afraid of you?" She clamped her mouth shut. "I know I am."

She poked the box into his chest. "Why are you talking? You're wasting your family money, too! Look what you inherited and what you turned it into. Half a store. Beat it. You can't help me, and I can't help you." She burst past him toward the door.

He stepped quickly to block her. "No."

She jabbed the box at him. "What do you mean, no?"

"First of all, running away is for losers. Two, where are you going?"

"None of your business."

"True, it isn't." He crossed his arms across his chest. "But the rent check. That is my business."

He's like a terrier, she thought. He gets one thing on

me and won't let go. "The campaign owes you, not me."

"Ask your buddy Brenda for the money. She'll be easy to find, she's probably with Rassy." If she'd been a cat, the hairs on her back would have spiked.

Kennedy tried to modulate her voice and failed. "I hate them both." You too, she thought.

"Maybe we can figure out some way for you to work it off." Chris relaxed his face. It's no fun getting dumped.

"No, I won't!" She tried going around him. "You can't make me."

He slid in front of her. "You will or I'll take you to small claims court. That would be embarrassing for your family."

"You wouldn't." Daddy will be furious. No, worse, he'll be embarrassed.

"Hey, I'm desperate here. I need the money." He reached for the box. "That getting heavy?"

She pivoted the carton away from his reach. "I thought you were selling the bookshop."

"I'm thinking about staying. I might as well re-expand and give it a last shot." He looked at her closely. "Selling out is for losers. It's like running away."

She thrust the box into his hands. "You want help from a loser?"

It was heavier than it looked. "No, I want the cash, but you don't have it."

She rubbed the feeling back into her arms. "You want to move all those books back to this side?"

He adjusted the weight in his arms. "Yeah. I'd hire movers like last time, but I can't afford it."

"Because I haven't paid you." She nodded. Like I'm the cause of your problem. "You also haven't sold many books. Enough books."

"True, but you have to admit, it's a tough business

climate."

"It's a tough political climate, too." He didn't move out of her way. "You won't let me leave until I work off my debt?"

He nodded, looking for a place to set down the box.

"Like a slave."

"Like a debtor."

"No, I'll just leave town." She aimed her best kiss-my-patootie glare at him. "What are you going to do, lock me up?"

"Nope, stocks on the Square. Maybe make a festival out of it. You know, DebtFest, or #IDontPayMyBills. We could get kids to lob rotting vegetables at you."

She thought that was kind of funny but kept the smile off her face. "What choice do I have?"

Chris set the box onto a chair. It must be full of rocks. "You could ask Daddy for the money you owe me."

"I'd rather die." She dropped down onto the office chair thinking how unfair it was. He played the Daddy card, but what would his own father think about him?

From the slump in her shoulders to the dispirited tone of her voice, he realized she meant what she'd said. "Well, at least you don't have to sleep in here anymore."

She raised her tired eyes. "I can't afford the BNB. That's why I moved out."

"There's an apartment upstairs." He gestured with his head. "Little bedroom, bathroom. Kitchenette. Small, not the BNB, but nice."

"There's been a bed upstairs all along, and I've been sleeping in here since the campaign quit paying?"

"You never asked." He shrugged his shoulders. "Well, it's there if you want it."

She raised her eyes shyly before dropping them. "Thank you."

"Bright and early tomorrow." He reached for the doorknob. "We begin Operation Last Chance."

"I'll be here," she said. "I've got nowhere else to be."

Chapter 41

When her eyes opened Kennedy had no idea where she was. The angles of the ceiling were obtuse, the wallpaper was wrong and the view through the round window . . . round window? She pulled the covers close around herself and slammed her eyes shut. Coffee? Who's making coffee?

Attic, I'm in the attic of the bookshop. My eyes are grainy, and I must have slept with my mouth open. She snatched her phone from athe bedside table. Nearly ten. I haven't slept that late in months.

She leapt from the bed and reached for her suitcase. Not there. It's Election Day, I have to get to work. She yanked the door open; her suitcases and her boxes stood at the top of the stairs. She pulled them inside and realized Chris must have brought them up for her.

The warm water of the shower both relaxed her body and freed her mind. It's not like I'm being held prisoner, she thought. I have nowhere else to go, and the price is right. That made her think of her father; it was one of his favorites. I'm not ready to face him yet.

She sluiced the crème rinse through her hair. Chris had left me alone to sleep. Brought my stuff up two flights of stairs and hadn't been a creeper about it. No, that's unfair. He's never been a creep, he's always been, what? She tried to think how he'd treated her over the years. She shut the water off and grabbed a towel. Thick and soft. Why don't I remember anything about him?

I can work with him a couple of days, get my act together and then decide what to do. She laid the blow-dryer on the small sink and pulled her blonde mane into a ponytail. It's gonna be a workday, so why should I bother fussing? She pulled on jeans and a long-sleeved Vuori, and noticed the fixtures in the small room. Almost as nice as the BNB. Up to my standards.

As if I can afford to have standards, she thought as she descended the staircase. The scent of coffee grew stronger with each step, her hunger as well. Maybe he has pastry, she thought. But that would mean the Gossip Ladies, and that was more than she could handle at the moment.

She paused on the second floor where she could see the campaign office below as well as the cramped bookshop on the other side of the partition. Bookshelves lined the walls around her, and she wondered why they weren't being used. Chris was moving around on his side of the wall, and she raised her hand to wave, but dropped it back onto the railing when he didn't notice her.

Election Day and the campaign office below her was empty. Should be bustling. I was in charge, the captain of a sinking ship. No, she told herself again, no. Scott chose not to listen to me. I was right, and he'll pay for it when he loses.

She looked from the failed HQ side to the bookshop side and imagined how the large space should be arranged. Maybe Chris will listen to me. He should, but Rassy didn't.

Damn that Brenda!

She walked around the partition and weaved through the stacks following the scent of the coffee. She found Chris behind his desk, a carafe, two mugs and a plate of Teddi's pastries in front of him.

"Have a seat." He grinned. "Get enough sleep?"

She took a bite from a bear claw before adding crème to her coffee. "Haven't slept that well for ages. Why didn't you wake me?" He held the mug so she couldn't see the dimple in his chin.

"Gonna be a hard day today. Lots of work, so I thought I'd let you sleep in."

Had he always had a dimple? "Oh, and thanks for bringing my stuff up all those stairs."

"Thanks for volunteering to work." He set down the mug. "You'll be needing all your energy."

She took the bite of her pastry and looked longingly at the plate. "Go ahead," he said.

"Nope, self-control is the key."

"Is that one of your father's aphorisms?" Chris arched his eyebrows.

"No, maybe an adage, but not an aphorism." She broke two fingers off the bear claw. "How'd you get these? Did you brave the ladies at the Pot & Flagon?"

"No way." His face opened into a broad smile. "I'm brave, but not that brave." He lowered his voice to a whisper. "I got there early. Before they showed up. Oh, and Teddi says hello."

Kennedy smiled back at him. "She is a sweetie. Why do you suppose she hangs around with those biddies?"

"Biddies?" He set down his mug and stood up. "I would have said shrews."

She furrowed her brows as if concentrating. "They don't look shrewish."

He cocked his head, then burst into laughter. "No, they don't. Hey, that was funny."

She smiled and stood up. "OK, so what's the plan today?"

"Simple, really." Chris stepped into the narrow hallway. "We take down the partition, re-position the shelves, open both doors and sell books."

"Wait," Kennedy said. "That's your plan? That's all you got?"

She had to step back as he returned to the cramped office. "Look, I'm not happy about it, but if I'm going to go down, if this business is going to fail, it's going to fail as it was. Both sides open, the way it was handed down to me."

She noticed tiny gold and green flecks in his brown eyes.

"Well? Is your highness on board with that?"

She shook her head to clear her mind. Weren't his eyes hazel? "Yes, of course. It's your family heritage."

He looked down at her skeptically. "It sounds like there's a 'but' in there someplace."

"I didn't mean it that way." She grinned and he didn't. "But I do have a few ideas."

He started down the passageway. "Whatever ideas you have, we need to empty these bookcases so we can move them."

She followed him. "You got enough boxes?"

"Tons. And tape. Everything we need." He turned around and squinted in the poor light. "Wait. Did you mean 'but,' or 'butt'?"

She laughed, he laughed, and they made their way to the fiction section.

An hour or so later, Chris placed one last book into the box and stretched his back. Kennedy had tied a kerchief around her head to ward off the dust and was filling her own box to transfer to the other side. He had to admit, she was a good worker.

She looked up at him. "What?"

"Nothing. Another couple of boxes and we'll be ready to start moving the shelving units."

She rolled back on her haunches. "Moving them back to where they were on the other side?"

"Sure, why not?" He wondered if this was when she'd start bossing him around. Like he was working for her.

"But why?"

He watched her stand and adjust her thin latex gloves. "Everything like it was before?"

Here it comes. He placed his box on the hand cart and reached for hers. "Do you have a problem with that?"

She steadied the cart while he stacked a third box on top. "Like your father had it, or your grandfather?"

"Can you handle the cart by yourself?" he asked and picked up a fourth box filled with fiction.

"Got it," she said and maneuvered the heavy load through an opening in the partition. "Over here?"

"Where the fiction section has always been." He dropped his box and pulled hers from the cart. When she didn't speak, he said, "Well, do you?"

He watched her swipe a hand across her face, and noticed she wasn't wearing any make-up. "I don't have a problem, you do." She spun the cart around and started for the other side.

At least I got some work out of her before she started on me, he thought. "OK, I'll play your silly game. What?"

She pivoted the handcart and sighed, dramatically

it seemed to him. "Why are we doing this?"

"What, this?"

He watched her nearly stamp her foot. This was what he was expecting. Another tortured sigh. "Did you sell a lot of books like this? Arranged like it was?"

Chris raised his open palms. She didn't wait for his answer. "No, you didn't. That's why you're in this mess."

"Yes, but—"

Kennedy took off her gloves and dropped onto an office chair. When he didn't move, she patted the chair next to her. "Sit."

This was more like it. "No."

She glared at him. He glared back but blinked. "I assume you have an idea."

She surprised him with a smile. "When you assume, you make an ass out of you and me."

He laughed. He didn't want to, but he laughed and took the seat next to her. "I'm all ears."

She grinned as if she were thinking of a comeback. "What has been your most successful way of selling books the last couple of months? Maybe the only marketing strategy that worked?"

"Chloe's Book Clubs."

She patted his knee. The only other time she'd touched him was the kiss. He tried to concentrate.

"Exactly. So, my idea." She turned and looked him full in the face. "If you want to hear it."

He pushed away the thought of how good she smelled after working all morning. "I always respect input from my employees."

"Employee."

He grinned, and she grinned back. "Go on."

"Yeah, so the only downside of Chloe's programs was the lack of space."

"We had to turn people away. A couple times." He thought for a second. "Your plan is to spread the books out and leave more space for people."

She beamed. He beamed back. "That's a good idea."

"We could offer Book Clubs for different ages. Teens and YA, adults. Or different genres. We could do romance club, or mysteries, whatever."

He found his hand on her knee. "And we don't have to move all the books back. We can leave spaces on both sides."

"Speaking of saving work." Kennedy removed his hand from her knee and said, "Can we maybe get Chloe and her buds in here to help?"

"You think I haven't thought of that? Like I don't have a plan?" He gestured with his hands to hide his embarrassment. "They'll be here when school gets out. Five of them, I think."

"That'll really help." She smiled at him, and he felt like she meant it. Then her eyes darkened, and he wasn't sure. "I think we should keep this quiet. Our new business model."

He brightened at the sound of 'our.' "What do you have in mind?"

"You got any old newspapers around here? And a couple of poster boards?"

Chapter 42

One of the essentials necessary for a democracy to survive is for the participants to truly understand the facts. While not every single piece of information is needed to render a just decision, the basic facts need to be ascertained and agreed upon, certainly before any action is taken. History records several unsolved mysteries, but for the most part the facts do come to the surface, are investigated in the clear light of day, and votes cast accordingly. For the Ladies Gossip Club of Benton Center, any missing facts are simply wedged into place where they seemingly fit, especially if they correspond to previously held notions.

"Kennedy fooled me, she really did," Mary Jane was saying the next morning from her place at the oval table in the bay window. "I bet you all thought the same thing."

"She definitely had a different attitude." Gena took a thoughtful bite of a bear claw. "Like she had grown up."

"Grown up colors, like a businesswoman." Mrs. Morse drew her eyes tighter together. "Not that childish bubblegum pink."

"From the first day she returned, remember?" Several heads nodded to Gena. "She came in here with her running clothes on."

"Presented herself like a lady on a mission. That she did." Teddi said. "I think she still is."

"What?" Gena and the others turned toward the barista. "You can't be serious."

"She closed down the campaign office. Yesterday, Election Day." Mrs. Morse nearly spat the words. "She quit, just like she did when she couldn't be captain of the cheerleaders."

"Did she leave town? I heard she's already left." Gena nearly smiled. "But maybe she's a book lover."

Teddi waited for her colleagues to calm down. "We don't know any of that for certain. What we do know is she was determined to manage the Rassmussen campaign by herself."

"And she failed. Rassy got trounced in the primary."

"Yes, Gladys, he did. But it seemed to me that he pulled the plug on her, and Miss Kennedy did not go running to her daddy." Teddi spoke slowly, holding their attention. "The important thing is, she did it on her own."

"She's still a loser." Mrs. Morse set her mug on the table with a thud. "So is the young man. His place has been closed for two days now. He must be selling out."

"It's been in his family for years."

"His father would be livid."

Gena waited her turn. "Grampa is the one. He changed the grocery store to a bookstore, and he must be rolling over in his grave at the idea. Selling out, with your own name over the door."

Maggie spoke up. "Gena, you don't remember Chris' grandfather, do you? I mean you're not old enough."

Teddi chuckled softly.

The mayor's secretary carefully laid down her sweet roll. "What are you saying?"

"Grampa Lennox died years ago. And you're not—"

Gena smiled slowly. "I think there's a compliment in there someplace." Mary Jane laughed, and the others relaxed. "No, of course not, I heard about him."

The door banged open, the bell tinkled and Sammi appeared at the table, out of breath and red-faced. "I heard something!"

The Ladies looked at the pregnant young woman expectantly. How could they not?

"I can't see anything, the windows are covered with newspapers, this high," Sammi stood on her tiptoes and stretched her hand over her head. "The doors are locked, lights are on. Both sides."

Maggie ushered Sammi to an empty chair and Teddi appeared with an iced latte. Decaf for the little one inside her.

"Take a breath, dear," Gena said. "And tell us what you saw."

"I couldn't really see all that much. At first." She swallowed some latte and let out a breath. "But it sounds like a herd of elephants is marching around in there. Thumping. Banging. Music playing."

"In the bookshop you're saying?"

"In both sides." The ladies collectively gasped.

"Something's going on in both sides?" Mrs. Morse shook her head. "No way."

"Chris and Kennedy are both still here? They haven't run away?" Mary Jane couldn't understand. "Neither one of them left?"

"That is very hard to believe, Samantha." Gena used her "I'm-the-Mayor's-Secretary" look.

Sammi re-arranged her place on the chair but didn't budge her report. "That's what it sounds like. There's a sign on the book side that says, 'Closed for Renovation,' and a 'Be sure to vote today' sign on Kennedy's side."

"You're sure there's activity on both sides?" Teddi pursed her lips. "That's interesting."

"That's not all." Sammi set down her mug and leaned forward. The others did the same as if drawn. "I went around back."

"Through the alley?"

Sammi dropped her voice conspiratorially. "By the loading docks, where they keep the trash."

"And?"

"I heard laughter." Sammi looked at their amazed faces. "Thumping and banging like in front, like they're working, but different."

"Go on."

"It's easier to hear in the back. The big loading doors are open. Hard to see with all the stuff piled up in back and I'm too short, but I could hear them laughing."

"Chris Lennox and Kennedy Phillips laughing?"

"No way."

"Laughing together?"

"Yes, ma'am."

"You mean laughing at each other," Gena said. "I can see that, they're both leaving town and they're blaming each other. Kids do that, you know."

Sammi stretched her back and placed her hands comfortably over her belly. "That's not how it sounded to me. They were laughing with each other. Like they were having fun."

Maggie patted her friend's hand. "We've known them a long time and that sounds . . . I don't know, weird."

Sammi's eyes widened. "I know, really. I have to

see what's going on inside."

"It's some kind of publicity stunt." Gena wiped a napkin across her lips. "Probably having a big sale to get rid of whatever he can before he sells."

"Then why do you suppose Kennedy is there? How does that fit?" Teddi's grey brows arched over her dark brown eyes. "She has nothing to sell, it's all campaign stuff."

"She must have a plan," Gena stared back at Teddi. "She's always been a planner. You know that, but Chris? He does everything by the seat of his pants. He's just doing what she tells him."

"He's followed her around like a lost puppy for years," Mary Jane told the Ladies.

Sammi furrowed her brows. "But why all the laughter? It sounds like they're having fun."

"Never heard them like that before," Maggie said. "She's always acted as if he was invisible."

"It's simple," Teddi said. "He's just happy to be in the same room as she is."

Chapter 43

Later in the week, the Election Day Disaster had been completely overshadowed by the Mystery at the Bookshop. Gena wielded the crème stick at Sammi as if she'd bought it on Diagon Alley. "That's it? That's all you saw?"

Next to her at the oval table in the bay window of the P&F, Gladys muttered, "Some spy you are."

Sammi's smile included those two and the other Gossip Ladies. She rubbed her belly and stretched. "Well, yes. The front windows are still covered, but they've done something with the newspapers."

"If you can't see through the windows, what difference does it make?"

Gena patted the pinch-faced woman's arm. "Go on, Mrs. Yoder."

"Right, so no, I can't see anything from the front, so I went around the back."

"Through the creepy alley?" Maggie shook her head. "Yuck."

"It's not so bad, but I didn't see much. Just bags of trash and a ton of Rassy for Senate posters."

"Rats?" Maggie shivered at the thought.

Sammi set down her latte and grinned. "A tough old cat, about as big as a Rottweiler." After the ladies gasped appropriately, she looked at Mrs. Morse. "I asked Rick and he didn't know anything, and since I hadn't learned enough the first time, I thought I should go back again myself."

"As well you should," the older woman replied.

"Yeah, so they've closed the big doors in back, so now that's closed off completely." She reached around to rub the small of her back. "Even you tall guys can't see in."

"But?" Gena jabbed the pastry at her again. Teddi sighed.

"So I went back around the front and found a small space where they hadn't covered the window completely." Sammi's expression changed, and she placed both hands on her baby bump.

"Feel anything?" Maggie leaned toward her friend.

"Nope, false alarm." Sammi's face brightened. "Too early, but I was hoping."

Gena laid down her sweet roll-wand and gritted her teeth. "You were saying?"

"What? Oh yeah. They've put some kind of posters behind the newspapers. Big letters on them, I think, so they can pull off the papers and have a message in the window."

Mrs. Morse tapped her fingers waiting for Sammi to raise her eyes from her belly. "What does it say?"

"No idea. Maybe the first letter is a 'W'."

"That's no help at all." Gena chomped the end off of her pastry.

"They're still laughing and talking inside, and music is playing. Whoever is in there." Sammi's eyes focused. "Oh, yeah, I did see something. A date and a time."

"For what?' Mary Jane looked the question to Gena.

"No idea, but it's today, this morning, at ten o'clock." Sammi slid her chair back and grabbed her purse.

"That's when your protest is, isn't it?" Mrs. Morse nodded to Gena in agreement.

Teddi said, "What protest?"

"We thought about cancelling it because they closed the store." The pinch-faced woman checked the time on her phone. "But we have almost an hour. I can get it organized again."

Teddi raised her voice a little. "What are you protesting, dear?"

Mrs. Morse spoke as if explaining something to a small child. "Smut, Ms. Burns. We are protesting smut."

"Pardon me?"

"Do you realize how many banned books they have in that bookstore? Hundreds of banned books full of smut, and anyone can waltz on in and buy them." She lowered her narrow face to her audience. "They can carry them out by the armload."

"They're going out of business." Maggie said sharply. "No one is flocking to their store, let alone clearing the shelves."

"But you can't see inside, can you?" Morse adjusted her coat and glared across the oval table. "Sammi couldn't, am I right? No one knows how many smutty things are in there. That's why they're banned."

"Banned where?"

Morse turned back to Teddi. "Does it matter? Banned is banned."

"As you well know, Gladys, there is only one banned book in Benton Center, that Seuss book, and it's only banned from the elementary library. Anyone can buy it."

"That's the problem! Anyone can buy smutty, banned books. Even children!" She took several quick strides to the door, then spun around. "I thought you people understood!"

Teddi stood and cleared the plates and mugs. "Sounds to me that our next meeting is ten o'clock at the Bookshop."

Inside the Bookshop, Chris and Kennedy watched a balled fist, then a coat sleeve rub a space clean on the lower corner of the front window.

"Would help if you'd ever clean the glass, sir."

"Can't afford it." He could feel her smile although she kept her face aimed at the glass. "But I have to admit it's a good idea."

"Another good idea." She nodded and kept her eyes away from his.

"Of yours," he added quickly.

"Pretty good for a loser."

"We'll see what happens in—" He checked the time. "A little more than an hour."

A little after ten, Teddi and several of the Ladies were perched on benches in the Square, enjoying the May sunshine and watching the book banners march in front of the Lennox Family Bookshop across the street.

"Do we need to join the crowd?" Mary Jane craned her neck trying to locate her daughter.

"No, there aren't that many people, and don't worry, Petey and the other kids are safe." Teddi pointed to the coffee shop. "We should wait for the big reveal."

Sammi nodded. "Looks like they're getting ready to pull down the newspapers."

Mary Jane gently shouldered the younger woman. "Like you can see inside, through the covering?"

Sammi giggled. "I got a feeling."

"Dear, it's the hormones."

"Another protester," Maggie said. "Look, coming around the corner."

"Now they have, what five or six?"

"Six," Maggie said. "Is anyone trying to get in? Are they blocking the door?"

"They were supposed to open at ten."

A dozen or so people had gathered in clumps at either end of the picket line. The Morses and their group marched back and forth holding cardboard signs. They were chanting something, but it was too faint for the Ladies to hear.

"Look!" Mary Jane pointed at the left-hand window of the former campaign HQ. Somehow the newsprint was being pulled away and large brightly colored letters emerged.

"What's it say?"

Maggie spelled slowly. "'B-o-o-k-s o-f a-l . . . Books of ALL kinds!'"

The protesters lowered their signs and looked at the slowly appearing message. The next window read: "Buy what YOU like to read."

Somehow the word had gotten out and the crowd was quickly swelling. Several cars were double parked and the through traffic ground to a halt. Behind the Gossip Ladies a steady stream of people hurried past them and across the street.

"The third window says, 'It's YOUR choice'." Sammi and the others stood up to see over the crowd.

"Look at the marchers. See? Gladys and her husband?" Maggie had climbed onto the bench. "They're blocking the doors."

"They can't do that." Teddi struggled to join Maggie

on the bench.

"They're linking arms."

"We should go over there and help."

"We can't get there, too many people."

"I can't see." Sammi reached a hand up to Maggie.

"Too dangerous," Maggie pulled her hand away. "We'll tell you what's happening."

"The fourth window is open. What's it say?" Teddi lifted up onto her tiptoes. Maggie steadied her. "Buy your books LOCALLY'."

"What's happening now?" Sammi waved her hands in frustration.

The crowd stopped moving and making noise. The doors of the bookshop opened, Kennedy stood to the left side, Chris to the right. Each beckoned the crowd to enter. No one moved.

"Now!" Mr. Morse said over the stillness. His protesters lined up across the doorway facing the crowd and locked their arms together. "No one may enter!" he called through his bullhorn. Behind the line, Kennedy and Chris waved their hands.

No one moved. No one talked. A long minute passed.

The middle of the crowd bubbled as if disturbed, and a handful of kids emerged from it.

"Oh, my God!" Mary Jane held her hands over her face. On the next bench Teddi shook her head slowly. "Your Meredith, my Petey and the rest of their band."

Mary Jane jumped down from the bench, helped Teddi, and the two of them made their way across the street and into the crowd.

In front of the doors to the Bookshop, Chris felt Kennedy's

hand in his. He pushed the protesters away from them. "It seemed like a good idea at the time."

Kennedy stifled a giggle. "We are attracting quite a number of potential customers, so yeah."

"Maybe they would be actual customers if they could get into the store." He extended his arm again to keep the protesters from being forced back into them. "Don't worry, the police will be here soon."

She squeezed his hand in reply. "They better be."

"No one may enter," one of the protesters shouted. Chris looked between the heads in front of him. It was Morse. The crowd was pressing forward, and he stepped in front of Kennedy to shield her.

There was a commotion somewhere in front of them. Chris couldn't see clearly, but someone was pushing through the crowd toward the protesters. Morse shouted again, and then it was quiet.

A small voice called through the stillness, "Hey, Mister! Can you move over?"

"No one may enter." Morse waved his sign over his head. The crowd rustled and murmured something the two couldn't understand.

"We need our sheet music." A girl's voice, more of a shriek. Chris spoke into Kennedy's ear. "Sounds like Meredith." Kennedy squirmed to see. "It is Meredith, and Petey, the whole gang."

Another small voice piped up. "Yeah. We need music for our band."

The Morses exchanged glances. One of the protesters lowered his sign. The crowd's murmur became a chant.

"What are they saying?" Kennedy peeked around the protesters. "I can't pick out the words."

Chris stood closer to her. "Sounds like 'Let Them In'."

She smiled up at him. "See, like I told you. It's a crowd of motivated buyers." She raised her fist with the beat and joined the chant.

The crowd chanted louder while slowly moving toward the protesters. The man who had lowered his sign turned slightly to face Morse, and a small space in the line opened.

Rick appeared in the opening and shoved the protester aside. "This way!"

Chris reached his arms through the line, and Petey and Meredith burst through. The little ones paused to slap Kennedy high fives and disappeared into the store. Chris and his friend held the space open, and the rest of the kids followed with a stream of onlookers on their heels.

Chris pulled Kennedy out of the flow and wrapped his arms around her. He kept them there as the crowd thinned, and the protesters melted away. She stepped out of his protective embrace as Teddi and Mary Jane appeared. "Tell the kids thank you," she said.

"Ten percent discount on all sheet music today." Chris waved to the Ladies, and Kennedy took his hand again.

Across the street Maggie stepped down off the bench next to Sammi, and they followed the crowd out of the Square. "That was great, but I don't get it."

"What's to get? The bookshop's open again."

Maggie stopped. "Are Chris and Kennedy working together? It looks like they are."

Sammi's eyes widened, and her jaw dropped. "No. Yes. Are they?"

Maggie took her friend's hand. "Let's find out!"

Chapter 44

Years later Benton Center remembered this event as the day they failed to stop reading. The first thing that struck the crowd as it burst through the line of protesters into the Bookshop was the layout, the way the books were stacked and displayed. Of course, the very first impression was that the space was not as cramped as it had been the past several months, and that was to be expected. But they quickly recognized the real difference.

Instead of being stacked in long lines like food in a grocery store, the books were grouped by genre in circles, labeled kivas. Rigid rectangular books shelves were not curved themselves but were arranged in arcs around central reading areas. Soft chairs and carpets with pillows strewn around made for pleasant places to open a book. Instead of the harsh lighting from fluorescent tubes in the ceiling, lamps of all sizes and shapes provided illumination.

The lamps didn't match a particular décor, but then nothing really matched. The only thing the chairs and sofas and settees shared was their heritage as refugees from an attic, garage sale or secondhand store. They were as eclectic as the bookshop itself.

Chris and Kennedy had changed the atmosphere of the bookshop. It felt more like a place to read books, than a commercial space to buy books. An informal place, a welcoming place, without the stuffy tone of a library. Talking wasn't forbidden, merely modulated, and the curved arcs of bookshelves served to stifle the noise. For a large space, the sound was more like a church than a big box store.

One of the kivas was designated for computers, and the walls there served to curb the clacking of keyboards. The machines were set on round tables, and patrons, mostly children but also many older folks, were encouraged to sit rather than lie on the floors.

Those who had followed Petey and Meredith into the revamped bookshop didn't realize what they were seeing at first. They wandered from kiva to kiva, marveling at the changes and asking themselves when all of this had happened. They scanned the shelves, grabbed books and flopped onto the furniture to open them. They showed them to the person sitting near them and without thinking about it, shared their observations. There were no librarians shushing them and it felt like the natural thing to do.

Maggie and Sammi took several steps into the former campaign HQ and stopped dead in their tracks. "What have they done?"

Maggi spun in a slow circle, letting the crowd flow around them. "This doesn't look like a bookstore at all."

"Or any kind of store," Sammi agreed. "More like a basement or a family room."

Maggie furrowed her brows. "Wait. All the people came bursting in here, and it's nearly quiet. No one's running around. They're talking in whispers." Her eyes flew open. "Wait, I am too!"

"Ooh, baby books!" Sammi grabbed her friend's hand and yanked her into a kiva with pastel-colored carpets and comfy chairs surrounded by childcare books for expectant mothers and easy readers. She pulled one from the shelf, rifled through the pages to a chart and showed it to Maggie. "See, six months, my baby is a as big as a volleyball."

Maggie smiled as she took in the bookstore. "When did they do all this?"

Sammi returned the book to the shelf. "They've been in here for two or three days. Windows boarded up. Must have been then."

"It's a ton of work."

"It was that." Kennedy appeared in the circular space and quickly hugged the two. "If Rick and Chloe and her softball buddies hadn't helped, we never would have made it. You like it?"

"Love it. It's so different."

Kennedy showed a bearded man where the Science Fiction kiva was, then said, "We had to change things up. Chris was going to sell out." She smiled and shook a tall woman's hand. "We may still have to sell, if this doesn't work."

"We? You've said 'we' twice now." Maggie arched her eyebrows.

"Do you have something to tell us?" Sammi leaned closer.

Kennedy blushed, said something unintelligible, and disappeared into the History kiva.

Maggie watched her quick exit, then said to Sammi. "I've never seen that girl blush."

"Not once."

"You two found the childcare section," Chris said with

a grin. "Got something to tell us, Margaret Mary?"

"No, I, um—"

"Sammi I can see, but you and Brent?"

Sammi recovered first. "No, you Mr. Lennox, you're the one with some 'splaining to do."

"Me? Whatever do you mean?"

Sammi waited for Chris' gaze to return from waving to a passing customer. "How did you two manage to do all this?"

"Whose idea was it?"

"Are you two an item?"

"Where have you been sleeping?"

Chris put up his hands to ward off the questions. "Chloe and Rick, hers, maybe and home. In that order."

"Wait." Maggie looked at Sammi.

Chris took Sammi's hand. "Come on, lots of time for questions, let me show you around."

Maggie grinned thoughtfully and followed them out of the arc of bookshelves.

Chris showed them the Mystery/Thriller section, the Cooking section and the Political section before dropping onto a sofa among the Romance books. No one else was in the rounded area. "OK, now I'll answer all your questions." He watched their expressions. "Questions about the Bookshop, not about my personal life." He smiled mysteriously. "Or Kennedy's."

Maggie gazed around the shelves. "Is this a hint? Where you keep the Romance books?"

"Maybe a Freudian slip." He rubbed his hands together. "OK, so the basic idea of the kivas, two ideas really, was to increase readability. Create fun spaces to read the books."

"Kiva? Isn't that a meeting space at Kent State? Brent told me that."

"It's from the pueblo people in the southwest. They're supposed to be lower than ground level, but yeah, that's where we got the idea."

Maggie nodded. "I thought so, but isn't the idea to sell books? Not just talk about them."

Chris shook his head. "Sure, the old idea. The idea that didn't work. The new idea is sales will follow the interest in the reading."

"The second idea? Yours or hers?"

"Well, Samantha, that came from Chloe, actually. From her Book Clubs for kids." Chris extended his arm. "We're planning Book Clubs based on genre. They can meet in the kivas and have their clubs right here."

"As long as they're here, they can buy the books. Clever."

"Hopefully, and the big space in front by the window will be used for book talks. Anybody can come in and use the space to discuss a book." He leaned closer to the two women. "Any book at all. In fact, Mr. Morse will be discussing *Green Eggs and Ham* next Thursday."

"He helped ban that book! He wanted to shut you down."

"Sure, and now we get to hear him explain why."

"But, that's—" Maggie's face opened. "Pretty smart. Get them in the store and sell them the kind of books they like."

"Yup, and guess who's scheduled for next Friday?"

Sammi practically screamed, "Joanie, or Sandra. The second-grade teachers!"

"Both actually." Chris beamed. "Excellent. They'll tell their side."

"And no matter who is on what side, you'll sell them a book."

"A gold star for you, too, Maggie. That's the idea.

It's their choice. Not mine or anybody else's."

"Got room for another?" Kennedy plopped down on the sofa next to Chris.

He patted her knee, then removed his hand. "Giving them the grand tour."

"Did you tell them about the book mobile, and Teddi's treats and the new webpage?"

"They're pretty self-explanatory, KK."

"Yes, but way fun. I'll go quickly. We deliver to your door, you can munch on Teddi's pastries while you read, and check out the webpage. Just hit the QR code on your phone."

"You don't have to do it now. When you get a chance." Chris stood and held his hand to Kennedy. "I'd better check and see how Chloe is doing. She's manning the sales desk."

"I'll come, too," Kennedy said and followed him from the Romance section.

"Did he kinda pull her along with him?"

"Hand in hand."

Both ladies knitted their brows. "Probably why they don't want to answer any questions."

Sammi sighed. "Any of the good questions."

Chapter 45

Teddi waited on customers at the counter while keeping her eye on the Gossip club table in the front window bay. When it was nearly full, she took a plate of pastries and a carafe of fresh coffee and joined them. Only Gladys seemed to be missing.

Before the barista could say, "Today's topic?" Sammi blurted, "They're in a relationship! Kennedy and Chris!"

Maggie tried to keep her friend in her seat but shook her head in frustration. "Take a breath, Samantha. The baby will pop out."

"And why is that so interesting, my dear?" Teddi had to smile at the two young people.

"Interesting?" Sammi's voice and pitch soared. "Interesting? They've hated each other for years!"

Maggie grabbed the back of her friend's jacket and held her down in the chair. "Baby volleyball doesn't like it when you hyperventilate."

Teddi set down her mug. "I thought they just

ignored each other."

"I saw them holding hands," Gena said. Beside her Mary Jane nodded. "Me, too."

"I saw them as well. Thick as thieves." Teddi paused. "That's not my point."

"My point is, where have they been sleeping?" Sammi practically bounced on her chair. "I know there's a bedroom upstairs, in the attic."

"That is interesting." Gena pursed her lips. "And they've had the place boarded up for several days."

"Nobody could see what was going on in there."

"Hold on everyone." Maggie shook her head. "Let's not get carried away. What they were doing in there was moving around all those bookcases and several thousands of books." She nudged Sammi next to her. "Even if they spent the nights in the bookshop, they were too pooped to participate."

"Too pooped?"

"My parents used to say it." Maggie grinned at Mary Jane. "I think we're getting ahead of ourselves."

"I agree." Teddi cleared her throat, and the group turned her way. "From what we've seen, there is some sort of relationship, Mrs. Yoder, but I disagree with the word 'hate'." She sipped from her mug. "In order to hate someone, you have to know them."

"They've known each other for years," Sammi said. "Since grade school."

"They have, surely. But did they ever really get to know each other?"

"What do you mean?" Maggie cocked her head.

"They have never been in the same group. She was always the golden child, and he was always in the background. From what I've gathered."

"No, I don't think so."

"She has a point, Sammi," Maggie said. "He followed her around like a puppy, and she never gave him the time of day."

"They had classes together. We were in classes with them."

"Teddi's right. Did you ever see them talk to each other?"

Sammi finally sat still. "Now that you mention it, no, I never did. It's like they were in two different worlds."

Teddi nodded. "Now they're spending days together. Hopefully getting to know each other."

"Like I said, a relationship."

"Sammi, we all know you meant a romantic relationship. That's not warranted at the moment."

"Theodora, I don't get it." Gena gave Teddi a quizzical look. "Three days and nights together?"

"That's enough time to get to know someone," Teddi said. "But not enough time to trust them."

Maggie nudged Sammi again. "Trust before participation, I always say."

Sammi slapped her arm. "No, you don't. I've never heard you say that."

The conversation stopped as Gladys slid onto the chair next to Mary Jane. "Sorry I'm late."

Mary Jane paused only a second. "Are you sorry about yesterday? I thought I'd lost my daughter in the melee. The melee you caused."

The pinch-faced woman took a calm sip of her coffee. "I saw Meredith inside and she was fine. Running around with her band buddies."

Mary Jane's face widened in surprise. Gena came to her rescue. "Are you ashamed that you tried to shut down the bookshop?"

Now Sammi put a restraining hand on Maggie's

arm.

"I am neither sorry nor am I ashamed, ladies." She looked around the oval table. "I am, or I should say I *was*, mistaken." She dabbed a napkin across her lips. "Twice, actually."

Sammi tugged Maggie's arm and the others remained silent. Mrs. Morse continued. "I thought the bookshop was peddling smut and I wanted to protect the children." She looked away and spoke in a softer tone. "I was wrong. I hadn't been inside the store for several years, and I convinced myself they were evil."

"You riled up a whole bunch of people." Maggie's voice shot across the table. "Someone could have been hurt."

"Thankfully not." Gladys nodded. "I was afraid. I thought they were forcing people to read certain books. The wrong books. Evil books."

Maggie opened her mouth to speak but this time Teddi glared at her.

Mrs. Morse swallowed a bite of donut "But they have no political agenda. They just want people to read what they want to read. Any book at all." She began to smile. "And the clerks, the young ladies who work there? I know several of them from the youth group at church. They're not evil at all, they're good kids."

Teddi checked Maggie's face, then said to the pinch-faced lady, "We are happy for you, Gladys."

"Oh, and the best thing." The woman nearly beamed. "They're letting us speak! My husband and I have a forum where we can explain our concerns about that *Eggs* book and others. People will finally understand our concerns."

Maggie sighed. "You're actually going into the lion's den? So brave." Sammi nudged her, and Maggie sighed once more.

Teddi waited for the group to listen to her. "As I was saying. A little knowledge of the other side." She looked at Sammi, "Like a little knowledge of the other person. That can lead to a closer relationship, or any relationship at all."

Chapter 46

The Ladies of the Gossip Club knew with certainty and felt with conviction, that good gossip was based on knowledge of the facts. After all, what good comes from expressing your opinion if you don't know what you're talking about? The facts themselves come from careful observation and thorough research, and with that in mind Sammi Yoder and Maggie Wellover had been commissioned to find out what was really going on inside the Lennox Family Bookshop. Could they verify that Chris Lennox and Kennedy Phillips were in a relationship?

Officially, they were chosen because of their proximity in age, but in reality Sammi would have had her baby on the spot if she hadn't been selected, and Maggie was the only one thought capable of curbing her friend's exuberance. As for camouflage in what was essentially a spy mission, they were provided with a tray of pastries and carafes of coffee and hot water for tea.

Maggie waited for a customer to leave and held the door

for Sammi with her backside. They acted as if they were supposed to be there, and in a sense they were. They set the goodies and drinks on the front table, cleaned up the crumbs and re-arranged the paper plates and cups. "There are so many people here," Sammi whispered.

"We're friends, we don't have to whisper." Maggie picked up a paper napkin and tossed it into the waste basket. "But yeah, a big crowd."

Sammi raised to her toes and spoke into Maggie's ear. "Where do you suppose the two love birds are?"

"Upstairs in the attic bedroom."

"You think?"

"Samantha, calm down. No, I don't think they are. Look. She's over by the computers and there, he's ringing somebody up at the cash register."

Sammi sighed. "So much going on, maybe we should split up."

"I can't trust you alone." Maggie took her by the arm.

The two pretended to be interested in technology books while observing Kennedy at a workstation in the Computer kiva. She appeared to be entering data from a clipboard on the table beside her. Maggie peeked over her shoulder: "Guest Speakers Calendar".

"You can get a better look if you come around in front," Kennedy said without turning around. "What are you two, spies or something?"

"We brought over another load of Teddi's treats." Sammi shook her head at Maggie's incompetence. "Lots of customers again today."

Kennedy grinned and hit the enter key. "Once it started, it hasn't eased up."

"You must be exhausted."

"Long days, but exciting." Kennedy pointed to the attic. "It's great to be able to just walk up those stairs and flop into bed."

Sammi avoided Maggie's glare. "We thought you had a room in the BNB."

"The campaign did, but I can't afford it." Kennedy flipped the page on her clipboard.

Maggie scowled at her co-spy. "What are you entering? Guest speakers?"

"I thought Chris had a good idea to offer a safe place for guest speakers, and it is, but everybody and his brother want to do it. We've had to set up a whole calendar, we have so many."

Maggie stepped in front of Sammi. "Anybody famous on the list?"

"Dr. Fine from the school board. A literature professor from Kent State. John A. Vanek He's a local mystery author. Oh, and John C. Bruening. He runs Flinch Books and writes pulp adventure stories. We heard the Morses are interested, too."

"Yes, we're getting a good cross section." Kennedy looked past the two. "And look who's here, the second-grade faculty."

Joanie and Sandra hugged the three and complimented Sammi on her baby bump. "We already signed up. We just want to check out the layout and see what it'll be like to present here."

"I'm glad you're here," Kennedy checked the calendar form. "Next Friday, right? Come on over and we'll take a look." The spies waved their good-byes.

On the other side of the curved wall of bookcases, Sammi whispered loudly, "She's been sleeping here for a week. Upstairs."

"She has to sleep somewhere." Maggie dragged her toward the check out. "Come on."

"He has to sleep somewhere, too," Sammi muttered.

The two spies had to wait for a break in the steady stream of customers before they could speak to Chris. When Chloe arrived, he was able to step away. The three flopped onto a davenport in the Sports kiva.

"It's good to get off my feet." He arched his back and sighed. "What can I do for you guys?"

Maggie glared at Sammi and spoke to Chris. "Is it going as well as it looks? There's a ton of people in here."

"Yeah, I thought yesterday was a one-time thing, but hey, it's a Thursday afternoon and the place is packed."

"Kind of a roller coaster ride yesterday."

"Sammi, we went from thinking we'd have to close, to worrying about a mob trashing the place, to having the biggest day—shoot, the biggest week—in years." Chris shook his head. "We are so fortunate."

"They're actually buying books, not just checking the place out?"

"I phoned in a re-order last night, and I'm about to do it again." Chris stood up and held out his hand. "She's the one to congratulate, they're all her ideas."

Kennedy slid into the kiva, and they kept their hands together. "Not all the ideas," she said.

He laughed. "No, we're a team, but just look at all the books. All the *types* of books they're buying."

"Everyone has an opinion," she said. "That's the point."

"Pick a book you like," he said.

"Or pick a book you can learn from," she said.

They faced each other and said together, "Just buy the book from us!" They hugged quickly and exited the kiva in opposite directions.

"I got him," Sammi said.

"I got her," Maggie replied.

Sammi found Chris back at the cash register. She waited for a lull in the crowd, nodded to Chloe and pulled her friend to the side. "We have to talk."

He saw the strange look on her face and led her down the hall to his office. "What's up?"

"Pounce." She calmly arranged herself on the office chair in front of the enormous desk. "It's time for you to pounce."

"What, uh, who, I uh."

"Kennedy. You. As soon as possible."

"I have to get back to work. There's a lot——"

Sammi settled her hands on her volleyball belly. "Sit down, Christopher."

Chris checked the hallway and slumped back into the old leather chair. "Kennedy."

"Kennedy."

"That has been my dream for, oh, you don't know how long."

"I have an idea how long, Chris." Sammi smiled. "Forever."

"Forever." His smile barely reached the corners of his mouth.

"Now is the time." She nodded across the desk.

"No, I can't"

She arched her brows and widened her eyes.

"Now that I can, I never could before, now that I can actually see it, see us, it's become, I don't know, precious."

"That's love." Sammi beamed.

"No." His smile faded entirely. "It's so precious and now possible, Sammi, I'm afraid to risk it."

"It's worth the risk, Chris." She held his eyes and

patted her baby bump. "It is worth the risk."

"What if she runs away? If I scare her away. I couldn't take it."

"That's always been the risk."

"No, before there was no risk, there was no way I could get anywhere near her. Now she's right here, and it can happen, and now." He raised his head. "It would kill me, Sammi. It would."

Sammi struggled to wedge herself and her baby to her feet. "You need her."

He met her eyes. "I do. I need her."

"Tell her."

Maggie found Kennedy in, of all places, the Cooking kiva. She watched her re-shelving books, and when the last customers left the curved space, she said, "What, now you're into cooking, too?"

Kennedy drew her legs up in an overstuffed chair and beckoned to the settee. "Too?"

Maggie turned and faced her. "Entrepreneur. Innovator. Working girl. Phoenix. Computers."

"That all?"

"I'm running out of words."

Kennedy's crystal blue eyes narrowed in suspicion. "Why are you here? You and your round fellow spy."

Maggie scrunched up her face. "No, that's not the question. For me at least." She straightened her face. "Why are *you* here? With Chris?"

The blond woman shrugged. "Got nowhere else to go."

Kennedy was a hard case, and truth be told, Maggie was a little afraid of her. "Bull. Crap."

"That's how it started. It really did."

"Come on, KK, you can live at home, or anywhere you'd like."

Kennedy realized she would have to give her something. Removing an invisible speck of lint from her tights, she said, "I didn't have any money. Rassmussen hadn't paid me in a month."

"Daddy's got money."

"He does, but I didn't want to ask him."

"Go on."

"There's nothing more to say, Maggie. It—it just seemed the right thing to do."

"Please. The right thing? Did you just invite yourself to stay, or did he invite you?"

"No, I don't know, we just sorta—"

"Darn it, Kennedy, you never *just sorta* do something. You always have a plan. What's your plan here? With Chris?"

"What do you mean?"

"You better not hurt him, Kennedy or I will track you down." Maggie leaned forward and bore her eyes into hers.

"Hurt him? I want to help him."

"Come on, KK."

"No, I really—"

"In your entire life, Kennedy, you have never wanted to help anyone. You have always been about you. Only about you."

Without thinking, Kennedy said what she felt. "I know."

Maggie stopped as if slapped. "You what? You're agreeing with me?"

"Self-centered. Guilty." Kennedy smiled weakly and raised her hand. "But Chris is different, and I'm different when I'm with him."

Maggie sat down on the edge of the sofa facing her.

"He's not like the others. All the others. Telling me

how beautiful I am. Telling me how to dress, how to act, how to be successful. How to make them look good."

Kennedy wiped a tear from her cheek. "He likes me without make up, in smelly old work clothes." Maggie reached for her hand. "He likes me for who I am."

"That's great, Kennedy. That really is."

"Yes, it is, but it's scary too."

Chapter 47

"Thanks, Chloe, Cathy. See you tomorrow."

The girls waved and disappeared into the darkened town. Chris smiled at their energy and positivity and wondered where he'd be without their help. Even so, they'd have to hire some full-time help. That good problem could be solved later; now he just wanted to get off his feet.

He found Kennedy curled into the corner of the sofa in the Arts kiva. Her eyes popped open, and she straightened up. "Hey there." He sat down next to her.

"Must have fallen asleep." She wiped a hand across her chin. "Sorry."

"Sorry? For what? You put in a long day."

"You did, too." She rolled her shoulders. "What's a phoenix?"

"A mythical bird or a city in Arizona. Why do you ask?"

"Maggie said something about it."

He looked closely at her, beautiful even in the dim

light. "The bird is consumed by fire but rises up out of the ashes to live again. It's a compliment."

Did he always have a dimple in his chin? "Great. I'm a burning bird."

"It means you're resilient. You overcome disaster."

"That would explain why I'm so tired." She smiled at him, and he felt it in his chest. "How do you know about the phoenix?"

"Better question is why don't you? We had it in English junior year." He grinned to soften his tone.

"I don't remember." She thought back. "Were you always this smart?"

"I don't know." He saw the light in her eyes and took another step along the high wire. "I only ever saw your beauty, your popularity. I never saw the real you underneath the glitz."

"What do you mean?" She watched his eyes dart away, then back to hers.

"Were you always so hard working? I thought people always did stuff for you, so you didn't have to." He watched her eyes narrow. Don't blow it! "These last couple days you've worked like a crazy person around here. Look what you've accomplished."

"People have called me a lot of things, but 'hard-working'? Not so much."

"It's hard being the Queen." He hoped he hadn't insulted her. He felt the wire vibrating.

Instead, she settled back in the chair. "Yuppers. That was me all right."

He gave her hand a squeeze and she returned it. When she spoke, her voice seemed to come from far away. "I was afraid to let anyone see who I really was. I was playing a role." She sat up and faced him. "You, Chris, I didn't know anything about you because I never looked at you. I never saw you."

"AYO's. I was one of them."

She opened her eyes in a question.

"All You Others, one of the invisible crowd."

"I was quite the brat." She'd tried so hard to be the wrong thing. "I didn't know what the phoenix was or what a kiva was, let alone who you were."

He stepped from the high wire to the platform. "But you knew what it felt like in a kiva, and how to make it work here." He waved to the re-imagined bookshop. "I had no idea how to use my vocabulary words. You did."

"It just seemed to make sense. I don't know how I knew."

"Doesn't matter. I needed help and you helped me." His throat tightened and he changed the topic. "And computer skills, KK, you got mad skills."

She warmed at the thought of him needing her but kept her tone light. "I thought you were the nerd. Turns out it's me."

They looked at each other, neither knowing what to do with their hands. Chris broke the awkward silence. "Did Maggie talk to you? Sammi talked to me."

"She cornered me in a kiva." She waited for him to laugh. "They're round, no corners. Duh."

"Good one." He gave her a wry grin. "She thinks we're in a relationship,"

Kennedy smacked his knee. "That's what Maggie said, too."

"Are we?" He wasn't ready for this. He could still blow it.

She watched his face closely. "Let's make a list, OK?"

He grasped the safety line. "Let's do it."

"Have we kissed?"

"Check."

"Have we spent nights together?"

"Does me upstairs and you on a couch down here count?"

"In the same building. Yup."

"Check."

Chris took a deep breath. "Are we planning a future together?"

She took his hand and gestured to the bookshop with the other. "Like this?"

He swallowed, afraid to open his mouth.

"Check."

"OK, then. Last question for you. Are you willing to take a chance with me?"

"I do." She giggled. "No, no I mean yes, I'm taking a chance with you."

"Me, too. Check, check, check." Without thinking, he reached for her, and she rolled out of the chair into his arms. "It's official, we're an item."

She nuzzled her face into his neck. "Can't wait to tell the girls."

"I can." He pulled her closer to him. "We have plenty of time for that."

Chapter 48

"I see our spies have returned." Gena tried to take a bite out of a jelly donut while talking and needed a napkin to cover the dribble. Mary Jane beside her pretended not to notice.

Teddi politely looked away. "I prefer the term research associates."

Maggie and Sammi settled themselves behind hot lattes and faced the ladies.

"Well?" Mary Jane looked at them expectantly.

"Waiting for Ms. Cobb, ma'am." Sammi demurely lowered her eyes.

"I can run to the counter and grab a towel." Maggie offered.

"I'm fine," Gena snapped. "Let's hear what you discovered at the bookshop." She dabbed the last bit of jelly from her chin.

"They're doing great." Sammi said. "Lots of customers, a steady line at the checkout counter."

"They've had to order more books twice since they

re-opened."

"With so many people in there you'd think it was crowded, but—"

"Stop." Gena held up her hand. "We sent you two over there to find out if they were in a relationship, and you bring us the Wall Street Business Report." She noticed a dab of jelly on the back of her hand and attacked it with another napkin.

"We were trying to say that with all the business, it was hard to get them to talk about anything else."

"Did you fail in your mission?"

"Not at all." Maggie smiled broadly. "We managed to talk to each one of them alone."

"We did." Sammi patted her belly and grinned.

"And?" Gena checked around the table to see if she was the only one not getting the message.

"I think yes."

"I'm not sure."

"It's complicated."

"Maybe you better come and check it out yourself."

Half an hour later, Gena and Teddi made their way down the street, the barista bearing a tray of pastries and her friend a carafe of decaf and another of high test. "If you want something done right," Gena began but Teddi shushed her. "Let's just see for ourselves."

A crowd of people was leaving as they arrived at the bookshop, and they waited as patiently as they could. The space was still rather full as they re-set the treats table and tidied the surrounding area. Gladys waved and hurried over to them.

"We just held our book club," she said. "It was great!"

"Good crowd, I noticed." Gena nodded at the pinch-faced woman.

"They were so respectful." Gladys lowered her voice as if sharing a secret. "They listened to us. Nobody yelled or smirked. I hate it when people smirk at us. Just because we have different ideas than most."

Teddi laid a calming hand on her arm. "There, there, dear."

"Thank you, Teddi." The book banner sighed. "It wasn't like on the street at all. No confrontation. Several people even wanted to join our group."

Gena looked at the three rows of chairs arranged in a semi-circle in front of the podium. "They listened? That's great."

"Yes, they did." Gladys smiled her crooked little smile. "And you know what? When those two second-grade teachers make their presentation, I think I'm going to come and listen to what they have to say."

"Amazing." Gena almost kept her disbelief from showing.

"That is wonderful," Teddi said.

"Now, if I can only find my husband." As Gladys disappeared into the kivas, Teddi said, "It really is a wonder. They're selling books and getting people to listen to each other."

"I suppose. It's interesting, but not what we came here to find out, is it?"

Chris gave the literature kiva a last look and stepped into the meandering hallway. Kennedy was looking across the floor at the two Gossip Ladies. "They sent another pair of spies."

"The big guns." He laid a hand on her shoulder.

She covered it with her hand. "Let's give them a show."

Teddi squinted, then pointed. "They're over by the literature books."

"They don't know we're here. Come on, let's see what they're up to."

The two ladies put down their cups and careful to keep their eyes off the suspects, left the speaking area and followed them through the winding pathways among the kivas. When the young people stopped, the old people stopped, sometimes grabbing a nearby book, other times faking a conversation or meeting a friend. Teddi and Gena were masters of deception and quickly fell into their familiar roles as researchers/spies.

Gena held out her arm to stop Teddi and peered around the wall of the mystery/thriller kiva. "She's in there. Sitting on the sofa." Gena pulled her head back. "I don't think she saw us."

A voice from behind them said, "But I see you."

They jumped as if tasered. "Chris, why are you here?"

"I work here, Ms. Burns. Ms. Cobb." He nodded to the ladies. "Looking for a good mystery?"

"We, uh, I, you see—"

He ushered them into the kiva and sat down next to Kennedy. She smiled radiantly. "Finding everything you need, ladies?"

"OK, you found us." Teddi flopped onto an overstuffed chair.

"Wait. What?"

"Sit down, Gena."

When they were settled, Kennedy waved a queenly

hand. "How are we doing?"

Teddi cleared her throat. "Looks like business is booming, and we just spoke to Glad—"

"No, us. How are *we* doing?" Chris took Kennedy's hand. "That's why you're here, right?"

Gena clasped her hands together in frustration. "OK, you caught us."

Kennedy winked at Chris, then bowled him over onto his back, burying him in kisses and squeals of delight. Gena brought her hand up to cover her face and Teddi laughed out loud.

Chris dragged himself out from the embrace. "Well, does that answer your question?"

Gena re-claimed her self-control. "You could be fooling us."

Kennedy kissed him demurely on the cheek. "Better?"

Teddi smiled as if this was what she'd always suspected.

"I have seen enough." Gena stood up. "I'm off to work, the mayor needs me." She bustled out of the kiva, nearly colliding with Chloe.

"Someone here to see you, Kennedy." The high school girl scanned their expressions if she'd missed something interesting. "In the office."

Kennedy disengaged herself from Chris. "You let him into the office?"

"It's, um. It's Mr. Phillips. Your father." She stepped out of the kiva as Kennedy rose.

Chris took her hand. "Should I come along?"

"No. I have to do this myself." Kennedy followed Chloe.

Chris looked at Teddi and leaned back into the sofa. "This could be bad."

"Maybe not." The barista took a calming breath and settled herself.

"No, it can only be bad." Chris pursed his lips. "I'm not worth it. He'll tell her to find someone with money and position, not a broke bookseller."

"Chris?" Teddi opened her face.

He looked away. "What was I thinking? I'm not in her league."

"No, you're not in that league. You're better than that."

His eyes darted to hers, then away. "He's here to tell her to get on with her life. I'm not part of that."

"Have you ever known Kennedy to do what other people want her to do?"

"With other people, no, but her father." His voice faded off.

"Chris!"

He looked up, startled.

"What's the worst that can happen? Even if he does say that, what's the worst?"

"It'll hurt like hell." Chris brought his eyes to hers. "It didn't hurt when I was invisible. We lived in separate worlds. Now, I've been with her, she sees me." His voice fell off again.

"'Tis better to have loved and lost, than never to have loved'." His eyes focused as he heard the words. She pointed to the bookshelf behind him. "Tennyson. Look it up,"

Chloe appeared. "You guys seen Kennedy? I seem to have lost her."

Teddi didn't turn to her. "Isn't she with you?"

"She and her dad are somewhere, now she's got a phone call. On the store line."

"Who's it from?"

"Senator Rassmussen. He says he needs to talk to her."

Chloe darted out of the kiva. Chris said to Teddi, "Great. That's just what I need."

Chapter 49

Kennedy had stormed into the office, grabbed her father's hand, and without a word, led him up to the balcony at the foot of the attic stairs, overlooking the bookshop below. They sat down on a bench next to each other but did not speak.

After a long minute, Grantham said, "All I ever wanted was—"

"For me to follow you into BiggInsCo."

"No," He kept his eyes on the bookshop beneath them. "It's your life. It's not about me."

"But that's not—" She stopped when he took her hand.

"Kennedy. You are really good about putting on a show for other people." He glanced quickly at her, then back to the activity below. "If you would be interested in the insurance game, I'd be ecstatic.

"Of course I would." Now he faced his daughter. "But don't do that for me. Do it for yourself if you want to."

"I could never see which way to go." She looked away from him. "I wanted to be like you."

"I know. You were only looking with your eyes." He slumped a little. "I wanted you to see the world with your heart, not with your eyes."

She nudged him with her shoulder. "If mom had been around."

"No excuses." He glared at the bookshop below. "I didn't know how to tell you."

She looked at the skin slowly healing around her nails and the unscarred pink polish on her nails. Outside the rain clouds had passed, the flowerpots in the Square were bursting with color, and Sammi's baby was on her way. Inside the reunited bookshop Chris was helping an older lady rise from a low-slung sofa in the Romance kiva.

"I was blind." She locked her eyes with her father. "I didn't see what my heart was showing me."

"You couldn't when your heart was closed."

"You should cross stitch that on a wall hanging, Dad." She hugged him. "But I see what you mean."

He looked closely at his daughter and cocked his head to the side. "So, you did all this?"

She wiped away a tear. "Who knew I could design a marketplace for books? I sure didn't."

"Then how—"

"I don't honestly know. I saw a need and it came to me."

"You opened your heart." Grantham agreed. "And the young man?"

"He helped me. We did it together." She looked deep into his eyes. "Chris helps me see myself."

His eyes retreated under his bushy eyebrows as if talking to himself. "Unlike the others."

"All those others. Yes."

His eyebrows rose. "He the one?"

She smiled. "Maybe. I think so."

He returned the smile. "A little scary, huh? To actually be there?"

"How'd you know?"

Her father took her hands in his. "I've been in love myself."

Chapter 50

The Phillips family found Chris and Teddi still talking as they entered the literature kiva. Chris sprang to his feet at the sight of the white-haired man, and Teddi followed suit.

"I'm just leaving," Teddi said and hugged Chris. In his ear she asked if he wanted her to stay.

"Gotta do this myself."

"That's step one." She smiled at him, greeted Kennedy and her father, and left the kiva.

Chris reached out to shake Grantham's hand. Kennedy's father furrowed his thick, white eyebrows. "I hear you want to marry my daughter."

"Daddy!"

"Well?"

"No, I mean, yes. Sure." Chris retrieved his hand and swallowed to control his voice. "But we're not ready now. We barely know each other." He winked at her. "But yeah, she's kinda cute."

Kennedy's father continued staring at him and didn't

exactly smile. "Good answer."

"There you all are." Chloe dropped her arms dramatically. "I've been looking all over for you. Kennedy. You have a call in the office. Senator Rassmussen."

"It'll wait."

"No, you should take it." Chris hoped no one could see the terror in his heart. He could feel Grantham's eyes watching him.

Kennedy followed Chloe out, and the two men sat down.

"Girl has to work on her priorities."

Chris nodded. You have no idea.

"Too damn squishy. I like 'em hard." Mr. Phillips tried to settle in the overstuffed chair. "You're sure about this?"

"I'm sure about your daughter; still working on the us part."

He lowered his eyebrows and Chris could barely see his eyes. "Take your time."

"I will, we will, sir."

Now Phillips cocked an eye. "About this Rassmussen fellow."

"Not a fan." Chris kept his hands from trembling. "He didn't treat your daughter well."

The big man didn't smile, but his head bobbed. "No, he did not."

Kennedy bounced into the room as if shot out of a gun. "Rassy wants to give it one more chance."

Chris could feel the blood leave his face.

"Says we can work it out."

"Young lady—"

"I told him he needs to write me a check." She saw the anger on her father's face and the dejection on Chris's. "I waited till the money was in my Venmo, then told him to drop dead."

"It's your rent money." She bounced down next to Chris and took his hand.

"Thanks," he managed, and the blood began returning to his extremities.

She put an arm around him and turned to her father. "Rassy's got money and good looks, but he's a loser."

Chris saw the smile break out on Grantham's face and let out a deep breath. "You're dumping him because he's a loser? What about me? I'm a loser."

She turned back to him. "I'm a bigger loser."

Grantham shook his head. "What?"

"No, I am. I lost the family business." Chris waved both arms and didn't notice Chloe and Cathy listening at the edge of the kiva.

Kennedy raised her voice. "What about me? I took the favorite in an election and turned him into an also-ran. I told donors *not* to give money to my candidate. I actually helped my candidate to lose."

Teddi had returned with Sammi, Maggie, Rick, and Mary Jane. They listened at the other edge of the kiva wall.

"You did, but I'm a bookseller, my family are all booksellers, and I have no idea how to sell books."

Chris was focused on Kennedy and didn't notice that all activity had ceased in the bookshop, and everybody was listening. "I agree, you are quite the loser. You could even say you lost the candidate himself to Brenda, right?"

"Yes. That makes me the biggest loser! The Queen of losers!"

"I agree." Chris lifted her hand high in the air and spun her around the kiva.

She stopped rotating. "Wait. What?"

"We seem to have gathered a crowd."

"We have." Chris waved to Maggie. "But they should know you're not actually the Queen."

"I could get my homecoming sash." Kennedy did the elbow wave again, like one of the Windsors.

"Actually, Maggie over there had more votes than you. She won the election."

Kennedy's hand flew to her mouth. "Oh, no."

"Yup. I mis-counted the votes so you could win."

"You did that for me?"

Sammi led a collective "awww".

"I thought that's what you wanted." Chris looked at his feet. "I loved you and——"

She pecked his cheek, setting off a louder "awww". "Why didn't you just tell me?"

"I didn't know how. Then." He took both her hands in his hands and looked her full in the face. The crowd stilled. "But I do now. I love you, Kennedy Phillips."

He pulled her to him in a warm embrace for maybe two seconds.

She extended her arms and pushed him away. "I really wasn't the Homecoming Queen?"

Chris swallowed his fear. "Nope. Never."

Kennedy looked around the silent kiva. Sammi gasped. Maggie furrowed her brow, Grantham slowly shook his head. Then she giggled. The giggle turned into a laugh, then a roar, then Chris laughed, then the whole room laughed, even her father sitting confused on the chair laughed.

"I don't have to be the Queen anymore! I never *was* the Queen! I'm a loser. I was always a loser. I can be who I am!"

The people watching burst into the kiva and Kennedy disappeared into an enormous hug. Grantham looped his arm over Chris's shoulder. "Took a bit of a chance there, son."

"Love is all about taking a chance, right?"

The old man nodded.

"Think it worked?"

"We'll find out soon enough." Grantham lightly punched his shoulder. "You did good."

Chris watched him leave, then extricated Kennedy from the cluster of people. "I love you the way you are."

"You don't really think I'm a loser?" She narrowed her eyes and cocked her head.

"Of course not. You got me."

She kissed him. "That makes me a winner."

The End

About the Author

David Allen Edmonds spent most of his working life teaching German at the high school and college levels. His summer jobs ranged from political campaign manager to stay-at-home dad to track coach. He co-wrote two educational TV series for the Cleveland PBS affiliate (WVIZ) and spent one summer in Hollywood on the writing staff of ABC-Paramount's *Out of the Blue*, a spin-off of *Mork and Mindy*.

He and his wife, Marie Mirro Edmonds, live in a small Ohio town with a Victorian gazebo and citizens who meet over coffee to discuss current events. He is working on several writing projects and wishes he had started his career earlier.

Visit him on social media or www.davidallenedmonds. com and be sure to leave a review at www.amazon.com/ David-Allen-Edmonds/e/B06XQN6HGQ/.

Acknowledgments and Thanks

There is no way this book would be here if not for the support, encouragement, and expertise of these people. I cannot thank them enough nor accord them their true value: Barbara Kauffman, Paula Lynn, Paul Kubis, Dr. Stacy Gnall, Rachel Fox, Kori Frazier Morgan, Connie Raybuck, Dale Chase, Heather Bayles, Sheila M. Cronin, Jimmy Brogan, Robert Allen Stowe, John C. Bruening and John A. Vanek.

Book Club
Discussion Questions

1. What was your initial reaction to *Unveiled Love?* Did you find it more of sequel to *Unexpected Love* or a stand-alone? How did Kennedy change or develop from one book to another?

2. Why is Chris so angry at Kennedy early on in the story? Did she treat him badly? Is he guilty? How does his attitude change? Why did it change?

3. Why do we label others during high school, and retain those expectations later in life? In spite of knowing how much people change as they grow older? And in spite of knowing how much of high school behavior is determined by peer pressure?

4. From your point of view, what were the central themes of the book? How well do you think the author did at exploring them?

5. How thought-provoking did you find the book? Did the book change your opinion about anything, or did you learn something new from it? Was it simply a get away from it all beach book?

6. Should the romance genre deal with heavy issues like politics and book banning? Should Romance remain light and escapist, or delve into current events? Is the genre a safe space from the pressures of daily life? Is dealing lightly with heavy issues a cop-out?

7. Is Benton Center too hard to believe? Do people you know act like these characters? Is it a stretch to think that a town can solve problems by working through them together? Especially in today's polarized society?

8. Who was your favorite character? What character did you identify with the most? Were there any characters that you disliked or found unbelievable? Why? With whom would you like to share a latte or glass of wine with?

9. Did you find the author's writing style easy to read or hard to read? How long did it take you to get into the book? Did you highlight or bookmark any passages from the book? Did you have a favorite quote or quotes?

10. Movie time: whom would you cast as Kennedy and Chris? Teddi or the Gossip Ladies? Scott Rassmussen? The pinch-faced lady?